Wishing to be
YOURS

Wishing to be YOURS

AJ RANNEY

Rudy House Publishing

Wishing to be Yours

Copyright @ 2022 A.J. Ranney

The book is a work of fiction. The characters and events in this book are fictitious. Any similarity to real persons, living or dead, is purely coincidental and not intended by the author.

Editing by Beth Lawton at VB Edits

Interior formatting by HC PA & Formatting Services

Cover by Taylored Designs

ISBN: 979-8-9859485-2-3 (e-book)

ISBN: 979-8-9859485-3-0 (paperback)

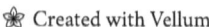 Created with Vellum

CONTENTS

For Christina, Natalie, L.M., Jenni, and Brittanee
thanks for taking a chance on me!

BRITTNEY

"March your uptight ass over to the bar and have a guy buy you a drink," Savannah said, crossing her arms and cocking an eyebrow at me. "If you don't, I'll make you sing karaoke tomorrow night."

Nope. No fucking way. My brother might've had the voice of an angel, but I sounded like a cat being skinned alive, and the little pain in my ass knew it. Savannah and her stupid bets.

"How—I mean—I've never..." I didn't know the first thing about getting a guy to buy me a drink.

My friends thought my lack of experience with the opposite sex was funny. I found it annoying. It wasn't purposeful, per se, but I'd spent the last eight years focused on school. I'd been in a couple of relationships, but I hadn't had time or the opportunity to do the whole single and dating thing.

Savannah laughed and shook her head before raising her shot glass in the air. "Here's to getting laid tonight."

She winked, and I struggled to remember why we were best friends as she tossed back her shot and slammed the glass down on the table.

I rolled my eyes at her before throwing back my own shot. It burned more than I thought it would.

"*You* might be getting laid tonight. I will *not* be."

A shiver ran through me as a chilly gust of air blew in from the lake. Even the heat lamps scattered between the tables didn't stop the cool wind from breaking through.

Savannah's gaze flitted back inside, scanning the patrons that milled around the bar. "Maybe some good dick is what you need to loosen up."

Rachel, a friend I worked with at the PR firm, giggled from the other side of our high-top table. We were seated at the edge of the patio, closest to the water. I couldn't argue with the need to loosen up. It was why I was here at The Silver Lining bar in Lake Tahoe. With my current stressful work situation, getting away was exactly what I needed. What I *didn't* need was casual, mediocre sex.

"I don't do random hookups. You know that. Sex is awkward enough. I can't imagine what it would be like with someone I don't even know."

"If sex is awkward, you aren't doing it right." Savannah shook her head at me. "I probably wasted a wish on you."

"What?" My gaze trailed over her shoulder to the bar inside. It was surrounded by walls covered with dollar bills. The idea reminded me of wishing on dandelions as a kid, putting a wish out into the universe and hoping somehow it came true. According to Savannah, a person puts a wish on a dollar bill and then pins it to the wall. When it falls, the magic of the universe will make it come true.

Yeah, okay.

Savannah was many things, and although sappy wasn't one of them, she was always rooting for the impossible. So believing in rare miracles was right up her alley. Me? I thought life was what a person chose to make it. The universe and magic had nothing to do with it.

"I was just telling Shawn—" Savannah started.

"Wait, who's Shawn?" Rachel glanced around, her attention darting from one man to another, reminding me of one of those bobble heads.

Savannah rolled her eyes in her usual dramatic fashion before running one hand through her short blond locks. "The bartender." She nodded over at a dark-haired man leaning over the bar talking to a guy in a suit. "I was telling him that Brittney *really* needs to get out of her head, let go, and have fun for a change, so maybe he could put my dollar up there gingerly."

"Hey, I have fun." Even as I said the words, I knew that in the last year or so, my life had been far from fun.

I'd skipped a bachelorette weekend last month because of work. And Savannah would *not* let me forget how much fun I'd missed while they celebrated her sister-in-law's final days as a single woman. Honestly, if Savannah hadn't planned for us to fly out on a Friday and fly back on Sunday evening, she probably wouldn't have talked me into this trip either. My job was more than demanding at times, and with the recent implosion of our owner's relationship, it was even more so. It had been hard enough taking the afternoon off to travel today.

Her eyes sparkled with mischief. "Since you're so good at having fun, you'll agree to my *fun* bet, right?"

"Bets with you never work out in my favor."

She laughed. "Yeah, 'cause you're lame. But if you win, I'll let you drag me on one of those hiking trails you wouldn't shut up about on the plane."

"Who comes to Lake Tahoe and doesn't want to take in the beautiful scenery?"

"Someone who wants to drink, gamble, relax, and maybe have no-strings-attached sex. That's who. If I wanted to hike,

3

I'd stay home and do that with one of my three siblings who likes that shit."

Savannah knew someone who'd rented a house here, and she got us a deal for the weekend. That was why we were here. She had no interest in taking in any sights.

We were different in so many ways, but she had been my lifeline when I'd had to start over in a new place and at a new school. My parents moved my brother and me from New York City to Half Moon Lake, North Carolina, when I was ten. Savannah was the first kid to befriend me on the playground. Her carefree personality helped me feel braver. She had a knack for pushing me out of my comfort zone.

Despite her best efforts, I always found a way back into that comfort zone. When was the last time I did something crazy? Something fun?

"I don't know—I just have to get a guy to buy me a drink, right?" I asked, determined to feed off her sense of adventure. I could let loose for one night, couldn't I? It was times like this when I envied her ability to let everything go and just be.

Her eyes lit up like it was Christmas morning.

Shit. What had I gotten myself into? "It can't be sex with a stranger. That's never gonna be me."

Her face fell, and she turned to look back inside the bar.

"Okay, fine." Her attention landed back on me. "You see tall, dark, and handsome in a suit at the bar? The one who's looking over here?"

I glanced that way, heat creeping up my neck and into my cheeks when I locked eyes with the gorgeous stranger. I nodded at my friend, wishing I could run away.

"Oh, yum," Rachel said as she too took in the sexy guy who continued to hold my gaze. "I'll take your place if you chicken out."

I sent her a glare. Why was I friends with these two again?

My stomach flipped, and my nerves ratcheted up a notch. What if the guy at the bar wasn't interested? Goodness, I'd gone up against my fair share of male clients, judges, and other attorneys. Surely, I could do this. And so what if he wasn't interested?

The cranberry and vodka I'd been sipping since we got here scraped across the tabletop as Savannah moved it closer to me.

"Liquid courage." She smirked.

I wrapped my fingers around the glass and downed the rest of the drink, this time savoring the burn.

I could do this. It was just a drink. And with a guy I'd never see again.

DEREK

THE DARK-HAIRED BEAUTY who held my gaze intrigued me. Most people tended to shy away from eye contact nowadays, their attention locked on screens more often than not. But not this girl. I was unabashedly checking her out, and still, she didn't look away.

She had an alluring look about her. Dark features and a tiny body that screamed to be touched. I licked my bottom lip and discreetly adjusted myself. I had finished up with my client today and wasn't due to fly out until early tomorrow, so I could indulge in a little pleasure.

I trailed my gaze from her black stilettos to her skinny jeans and a tight black tank with thin straps. The top was sparkly and scooped low, giving a nice peek of her tits. It probably did nothing to combat the chilly September air.

She brought the glass of pinkish liquid to her mouth and threw it back in one gulp. Something about her had caught my attention the minute she walked in an hour ago, and I hadn't been able to take my eyes off her since. She zeroed in on me again as she moved away from her table and walked in my direction. I'd never prayed to a god before, but damn did

I want to fall to my knees and pray her intended destination was me.

I brought my drink to my mouth as she shimmied up to the bar next to me.

"Hi," she said and finally broke eye contact by glancing down between us. Was she nervous? Or maybe shy? She'd kept her focus fixed on my face the whole way over, but now she was looking anywhere but at me. That intrigued me even more.

Women who approached me at bars typically did it with an air of self-confidence, some even offering to buy *me* the drink. It made it easy. Two people looking for nothing but a shared night of pleasure. It didn't always end up that way, one of us walking away for whatever reason, but the cards were usually on the table and intentions were clear. But I had no clue what this girl's intentions were. I'd be lying if I said I didn't want to be inside her, which was usually the only thing I cared enough to work for.

I'd tried the dating and relationship thing a handful of times, and I didn't have the energy to do it again, so over the last year or so, I'd stuck to casual hookups. For some reason, I attracted high-maintenance women. I was convinced the type of woman I needed didn't exist. Why was it so hard to find a woman who wanted an equal partner rather than someone to take care of her?

"Hey." I couldn't explain why I didn't mind the idea of just talking to this chick. "Can I buy you a drink?"

Her eyes widened, and I had to bite back a laugh. She obviously didn't know what to do or how to respond. But she squared her shoulders and nodded. It was refreshing how easy she was to read.

I flagged the bartender over, ordering each of us one of their signature rum runners.

"So...do you come here often?" she said before she

cringed and pinched the bridge of her nose. "Wow, I suck at this. That was totally cliché." An awkward chuckle escaped her kissable lips.

I threw my head back and laughed. "Well, I did start with the classic 'can I buy you a drink?'"

She relaxed a bit, and her smile grew. "Yeah, you did."

The bartender delivered our drinks, fighting back a laugh of his own, if the grin on his face was any indication.

"How about we start over?" I handed over her drink and watched as she brought the straw to her lips and took a sip, her eyebrows rising. "Hi, I'm Derek."

"I'm Brittney, and my friends are right. I'm lame," she pouted.

I fixated on that plush bottom lip, wondering what it would taste like. "I doubt you're lame. You're so gorgeous you must spend all your time fighting off the advances of every man you come into contact with. I bet you rarely need to make the first move. And frankly, if you hadn't come over to me when you did, I would have walked over to your table."

She arched her eyebrows as her eyes popped open wider. She shook her head. "See, that's where you're wrong. I don't go out very often. Only for the occasional happy hour with my coworkers."

"Oh?" A hint of jasmine hit my nose as I leaned closer. "But I wasn't wrong about you being gorgeous," I whispered as I brushed my hand along her arm, eliciting a shiver from her. "Are the girls who keep staring at us your coworkers, then?"

She swiveled to send a glare their way. They both laughed, the tall blonde sending her an air kiss in response. "She won't be laughing tomorrow when I make her hike five miles," Brittney mumbled.

"Huh?"

"The blonde is my best friend, Savannah, and the redhead

is a friend I work with. I'm making them go hiking with me tomorrow. Savannah's not very outdoorsy."

"Check out Inspiration Point, it's a must. Beautiful view."

She smiled into her drink, as if she was surprised by my answer.

"So, uh—you're from around here? That's what I was trying to get at earlier with my cliché question."

"Nah, I live in Nashville. But I have a client who lives here, so I come out every now and then to deal with his messes."

She widened her eyes again. Would those deep brown orbs pop open in surprise when she came?

I shook my head at the thought; that was probably not where this was going. "I'm a trail runner, so I take every opportunity I can to run new and challenging trails."

"I don't run trails. I'd probably fall on my ass. I enjoy hiking though." She tucked a piece of hair behind her ear before glancing at the small group of couples dancing to the music. "You said you had a client here? What do you do?"

"Public Relations."

She shot her gaze back to mine before she laughed.

"Of course you do," she said as she shook her head. "I work for a PR firm."

Interesting. I tried not to label women, but she seemed young—obviously at least twenty-one—but she couldn't have been much older than that. Maybe she was an intern or an assistant. Before I could ask, her blond friend—Savannah, I think she called her—stepped up behind Brittney.

"We want another shot. Does Mr. Hot as Fuck want to join us?" She sent me a wink, then waved over the bartender as I huffed out a chuckle. "Shawn, can we get another round of shots?"

I loved coming to this bar when I was in town. It was laid back, with just the right mix of locals and tourists. I'd been here more often recently, dealing with my client, Jasper, and his mess of drugs and prostitutes. We'd had to stop sending our female reps because he would harass them, and frankly, I was done dealing with him as well. I'd made it very clear today that if he didn't at least try to stay out of the press, there wasn't much more I could do for him.

After Brittney officially introduced me to Savannah, I followed them back to the table and met the redhead, Rachel. The four of us downed our shots, and not fifteen minutes later, I was sent to the bar to get another round.

After throwing back the next shot, Savannah dragged Rachel onto the dance floor. There was just an acoustic guitarist playing from the small stage on the far side of the bar, but that didn't stop people from swaying along to the music.

I caught Brittney looking at me, so I leaned over, my mouth close to her ear, and put my hand on the small of her back.

"Wanna dance?"

She gave me a slight nod, and I led her onto the dance floor, pulling her close to my body. Across the open space, she and Savannah exchanged looks I wished I could decipher. Brittney's eye roll and shake of her head sparked my curiosity.

The sexy gasp that left her mouth when I spun her around so her back was pressed tightly against my front immediately made my dick take notice. And fuck me. She didn't miss a beat with a slight twerk of her ass against my hardening cock. More than likely, I'd end up with a painful case of blue balls by the end of the night, but at the moment, I didn't give a damn. She had me hooked; and I'd gladly take what she was willing to give.

I ran my hands from her arms to her stomach, down to right below her hips as we moved along to the beat.

"You're so fucking sexy," I whispered, my lips grazing her outer ear. I swear I heard her moan.

"I bet you say that to all the girls you pick up in bars." She tilted her head and looked at me over her shoulder.

It took everything in me to pull my attention from her mouth as her tongue traced along her bottom lip.

"Nope, most of them try too hard. You don't even realize you're being sexy. Do you?"

She widened her eyes again. Just as I'd suspected; she had no clue just how sexy she was.

This time, the words left my mouth before I could stop them.

"I wonder if that's how you'd look if you were under me."

Truthfully, I was surprised I didn't get slapped.

Instead, she grinned. "I don't put out on the first date."

"Good thing this isn't a date then."

When she leaned back into me, I had to know if I had any chance. I inched my mouth closer to her, giving her a chance to pull away. But she didn't. Once our lips met, I craved better access to deepen the kiss.

Spinning her in my arms, I tangled one hand in her hair and pressed her center tight against my thigh. I traced the seam of her lips with my tongue, demanding entrance as we continued to move against each other in time with the music. She broke the kiss with a sharp intake of air, and I smirked, noticing her movements against my thigh were getting insistent.

Maybe I had read her wrong. Maybe this night would end with me inside her after all.

BRITTNEY

WHAT THE HELL was wrong with me? I was literately rubbing myself against some stranger's leg like a dog in heat. How embarrassing. It *had* been almost a year since I had been with someone, but still. When I looked into Derek's dark green eyes, though, I saw the same passion blazing back at me. I shouldn't be surprised; his erection was currently digging into my hip, so I wasn't the only one feeling this intense attraction.

I didn't do this type of stuff though. I'd lost my virginity to my high school boyfriend. I dated someone else briefly in college. And in law school, I dated someone seriously, but we'd broken up last year. None of my relationships had ended horribly, they just didn't work out. My most recent breakup had been complicated because we'd lived together, but it had still ended amicably. He just couldn't handle someone as career oriented as me. He needed a partner who wanted to be a housewife, and that wouldn't ever be me. I was also only twenty-five; I wanted to live life, maybe travel, before having kids.

"Don't," Derek mumbled into the space between us.

"What?"

"Don't overthink this." He searched my face like he was trying to figure me out.

Yeah, good luck with that. I wasn't even sure who I was at the moment.

"I just… don't do this."

"I gathered." He trailed his hand from the back of my head down my spine, skimming his fingers just under the waistband of my jeans.

I couldn't stop the shiver that rocked through me at his touch. And it didn't escape me that he was a perfect stranger, yet the guy I'd dated for over a year didn't even have this effect on me. Regardless, I wanted this. Oh my god, did I want it. Or rather, my body wanted what he was offering.

When he started to move me against his thigh again, I narrowed my eyes at him.

"Are you trying to seduce me?"

"I didn't think I was being subtle about that. Is it working?"

His hold-nothing-back honesty reminded me so much of Savannah. I swallowed, realizing I might just be willing to do this.

"You know it is."

His victorious smirk and the slow movement of his thumb against my bare skin sent another shiver through me.

"Do you, um, want to walk me back?" Had I seriously just invited a perfect stranger to take me home? I watched enough horror movies and *Dateline* to know this was how people ended up dead. I swallowed, my throat suddenly dry.

Derek leaned down and brushed his lips against my ear before whispering, "Yes. Very much. But I can tell you're already regretting that offer."

Was I *that* obvious, or could he just read me *that* well? I wasn't regretting my offer though. I definitely wanted to experience this. However, my subconscious was screaming that this wasn't me. Could I possibly not be me for one night? Would he stay the night? Would we get breakfast together tomorrow? I had so many questions.

"I've never—you know... hooked up with a random stranger. Are there rules? Like will you stay the night?"

"It depends. Sometimes, yes. Other times, no. Do you want me to stay the night?"

I nodded. Afraid I would say something else embarrassing to show my lack of experience.

"Then I will."

Before I could ask another inane question, Savannah brushed past, stopping briefly to whisper in my ear. "Your girl can't hold her liquor. Taking her back. You good?"

I nodded. "Yeah. Want me to come with?"

"Nah, I got this. You stay with Mr. Hottie." Savannah winked before walking away.

Another rum runner and an hour later, Derek and I were crashing into the small bedroom that was mine for the weekend. I couldn't explain it—I was desperate for him. Desperate for the way his hands caressed me, and how sexy he made me feel.

It wasn't just that. He didn't rush; he didn't just chase his own release the way my past partners had. He kissed me and explored my body. Making it respond, making *me* respond in ways I hadn't in a long time. And by the time he was sinking into me, all my reservations were gone, replaced by a need for the pleasure he was giving me.

It was nothing like I expected a one-night stand would be. It was so much more. And when he played with my hair as I fell asleep on his chest, I knew I was smiling like an idiot.

It wasn't until the next morning, when those reservations came back at full force, that I realized Derek had snuck out sometime in the middle of the night. I knew the score, but I figured he'd have the decency to hang around in the morning and say goodbye. Was I imagining things, or hadn't I specifically asked if he would stay the night? He *did* say yes, right? Was that just a line he fed all the girls?

I stretched in the small bed, listening to the chirping of the birds outside the window and Savannah and Rachel's laughter from the shared kitchen. The smell of bacon and coffee was enough motivation to swing my legs over the side of the bed and get dressed. I couldn't hide in my room all day; it was time to face the inquisition.

Was I hoping Derek felt the same connection I had? Of course, but I wasn't naive. At the very least, he could have left me a note. He hadn't come off as a complete player, but I guess I was wrong. He told me what I needed to hear to be comfortable enough to sleep with him, and he knew it.

Whatever. One good thing had come from the whole experience. Well, two, if you count the toe-curling orgasm he gave me last might. Too bad he had the personality of a snake. But Savannah has to hike with me, and listening to her moan about her legs, her hair, and the bugs should be enough to cheer me up. Time to put Derek the Douche out of my mind. Thankfully, I'd never have to see him again.

4

DEREK

"DEREK, you're saving my ass here. Don't ever work with your wife, especially if she's the head of legal. She'll take you for everything you're worth in the divorce," Hunter said as we stood in the lobby of the building where his PR firm was located.

I'd started working for Hunter and his brother Liam straight out of college eight years ago. When Hunter got married, he and his wife took over the Asheville location. Meanwhile, Liam opened a second firm in Nashville, taking me along with him as his right-hand man.

"Hopefully everything gets resolved quickly and amicably," I said, crossing my arms over my chest, ready to get upstairs and dive into my new position. *Temporary* position. I didn't plan to stay. I liked my job in Nashville and was already itching to get back.

Hunter scoffed like that was the craziest thing I'd ever said. "If Meredith has her way, this will be long, drawn-out, and torturous."

I had to bite back the retort on the tip of my tongue. Liam had spared no details over the last few months about the drama unfolding between them. Neither was innocent, and they'd both played an equal part in the demise of their marriage, at least from Liam's perspective.

I couldn't say no when Liam asked me to step into the role of president of operations of this location so Hunter and his soon-to-be ex-wife could take a step back. The nasty divorce was getting too much attention from the media. Meredith was from a wealthy and well-known family in Asheville that owned several of the major corporations in the city. So the media had latched on to the drama pretty quickly.

I followed Hunter through the lobby and into the elevator. He spoke again once the doors had closed.

"Legal and HR are waiting for you. They'll get you set up with nondisclosures and any other paperwork they might need. I'll leave you with them, and they can get you squared away in your office. I have an appointment with my attorney."

I nodded. It had been five years since I'd worked in this office. Meredith was the only one in legal at the time, and an older woman ran HR on her own back then, so I had no clue who I was getting handed off to.

My phone buzzed in my pocket as we exited the elevator and passed the receptionist's desk. I pulled it out, dismissing Liam's call. I'd talk to him once I got all the paperwork out of the way.

This office was set up differently than the one in Nashville. As I followed Hunter, I scanned the space, taking note of the individual offices that lined the outside and the cubicles filling the space in the middle.

I made a sharp left into an office behind Hunter and came to a dead halt.

No fucking way.

My dick was already perking up, recognizing this year's

best lay. I quirked my lips in a grin but quickly schooled my expression when I noticed her glare.

"You." Brittney's barely audible word sliced through the air.

I glanced over my shoulder, expecting to find some asshole behind me. If her face was any indication, she hated the poor dude. Her tone, a mix of anger and disbelief, was almost worse than her glare. And yet I was more shocked that the space behind me remained empty.

I turned back and was met with dark brown eyes that narrowed right at *me*. Me? I was the asshole she was glaring at? What the fuck was she so pissed about? I'd left her more than satisfied that morning in Lake Tahoe two weeks ago, hadn't I? In fact, I was sure I had. I wasn't that rusty, nor was she any type of actress. So what the fuck was going on?

None of my runaway thoughts stopped my gaze from roaming down Brittney's body covered in a sexy pants suit. Nor could they stop me from remembering just how responsive that little body was. No. No way she faked that shit.

"Well, this just got interesting."

My head swiveled to the left, taking in the way the redhead cocked an eyebrow as she glanced from Brittney to me.

"Wait, you already know each other?" Hunter's confused expression made me realize how precarious our situation had just become. It was frowned upon to fuck employees, despite how much I wanted round two, or maybe three, with Brittney.

Rachel, the redhead from the bar that night, stole another glance at Brittney, who was still shooting daggers in my direction. It took every ounce of control I had not to ask her why the hell she was so mad.

None of us spoke for what felt like an eternity.

Finally, Brittney let out a breath and said, "We've met.

Doug, was it?" She arched an eyebrow, and without waiting for a response, added, "Or was it Dennis?"

She'd had no problem remembering my name when she was moaning it over and over as I made her come. I bit back a smirk; two could play at this game.

"Hmm. Brenda, right?"

Her eyes blazed at my response. Oh, so she could dish it out, but she couldn't take it.

"Well, since you all know each other, this should go smoothly."

Smooth? This dumbass was the one Brittany should be glaring at. How did Hunter get smooth from the exchange that had just taken place? We didn't even use the correct names for one another. I stared at him, but he just smiled, oblivious to the tension filling the room.

"On that note, I gotta run. Late for my appointment." He turned and strode for the door.

Once Hunter had left the office, Brittney and I continued our staring contest, neither saying a word until the sound of a throat clearing broke the tension.

We both turned our glares to Rachel.

"Should we, um, get this paperwork done? Or do you two need a minute?"

"We need a minute," I said at the same time Brittney said, "We *do not* need a minute."

Brittney crossed her arms and narrowed her eyes in my direction once again. "We're going to do our jobs. Nothing else."

I almost asked, *are you sure nothing else?* But no, I did not. I was her boss now. She was right. We had to work together and be professional.

So my dick just needed to shut the fuck up.

Brittney

HUNTER JUST LEFT. Like everything was all sunshine and rainbows. Had he totally missed the vibe in here? He really was an *idiot*. Regardless, I wasn't sure I could work with Derek the Douche for the next few months. But I had no choice. I couldn't let Meredith down. I knew she wasn't innocent in all the divorce drama, but I'd promised her I would step into her shoes and make sure this place didn't crash and burn.

I'd been telling her constantly over the last year to end things amicably with Hunter. But her dramatics just delayed the inevitable, and now they were working to destroy one another. And in the midst of all that, my own drama had shown up.

What were the chances that the guy I had my first, and *only*, one-night stand with would end up being my boss? I didn't know if I was angry or humiliated or both. I knew the person they were sending was Liam's vice president of operations at the firm in Nashville, but—wait a minute…

"Your name is Eugene." I pointed to the nondisclosures he was signing. I hadn't made the connection because all the paperwork Rachel and I put together was for a Eugene, not a Derek. So he lied about his name too when he was feeding me all his bullshit.

What a jackass.

He looked up, one brow arched, like he was trying to relay something I didn't give a fuck about. Yeah, he should feel like an ass.

"Eugene is my given name. I rarely use it. I go by my middle name—Derek."

His phone vibrated against the desk where he'd set it while he signed the documents. He dismissed the call and placed the phone back in his pocket. Interesting. Who was on the other end of that call? Did he have someone back in Nashville? I swallowed the bile that rose at the back of my throat at that thought.

He finally looked up after signing his name on the last signature line. "So, you're head of legal, and Rachel, right?"— he glanced over at Rachel and continued when she nodded— "Is HR?"

I crossed my arms, ready to get him the hell out of my office.

"Yeah. I'm stepping into Meredith's role while she and Hunter deal with the divorce crap."

"You're young," he had the nerve to say.

I raised my eyebrows at him. The urge to scream was strong. Why did everyone always judge me based on my age?

"I'm smart and determined; age doesn't affect that."

"I was simply making an observation."

"My age wasn't an *observation* when you—"

Keep it professional. I can't and won't let this stop me from doing my job.

I swallowed and gathered the documents that sat on my desk.

"Rachel and I will get this squared away. Just let us know if you need anything. Kayley will show you to your office." I pressed the button on my phone to connect me to Hunter's annoying assistant.

"Who's Kayley?" Derek, or whatever the fuck his name was, looked between Rachel and me. I should start calling him Eugene. That might make me feel better. It actually just annoyed me more that he was too good looking to be a

Eugene. I wished he'd had a name like Tad or Brad. Something fitting of his personality.

"Your assistant." I nodded to Kayley, who had stepped into the doorway.

His head swiveled to her, then to Rachel, before he turned back to me.

"Am I the only one in the office over the age of twenty-three?"

I rolled my eyes. "No. We have a staff meeting scheduled for tomorrow morning. You can ask everyone their ages then if you'd like. Now, if you'll excuse me, I have paperwork to file."

He narrowed his eyes, but I held his gaze. I wasn't about to let him see how ready I was to lock myself in my office and never come out.

Fake it till you make it. That was the saying, right?

I could do this. It was only for a few months.

5

DEREK

VERY QUICKLY, my assistant proved to be utterly useless. Why the hell had Hunter hired her? She was young and pretty, but would Hunter really hire someone so inexperienced just because she was easy on the eyes? Meredith had accused Hunter of cheating, so I hoped this girl hadn't gotten mixed up in that.

I could see Brittney's patience dwindling each time she was summoned to help Kayley with something.

My cell vibrated against the desk, pulling me from my thoughts. Liam hadn't picked up when I called him back, so I was relieved to see it was him.

"Hey," I said once I answered his call.

"Do not ever go into business with a spouse, or date someone you work with, for that matter. This is such a fucking mess, and my brother is a complete and utter idiot."

My mind immediately went to Brittney. No fucking clue why. Even if she was game, which I doubted, based on her reaction, I had no interest in getting serious with anyone. Especially someone I worked with, temporary or not. Once this whole thing was over, I'd be back in Nashville, and she'd be here.

"Yeah, he seemed over all the divorce drama when I talked with him earlier."

"Sometimes I wonder if we're actually related. He still blames Meredith for everything that went wrong in their marriage. She was so focused on her career and this firm that she neglected him. He blames her dramatics for every disagreement or problem. Like he didn't make any mistakes along the way."

I chuckled. Times like these, I was glad I was an only child. I changed the subject, ready to move on to anything that didn't revolve around Hunter's divorce, and we talked for another ten minutes about work stuff and how I was settling in.

"I temporarily reassigned most of your clients here, but you have to keep Jasper. No one here is willing to work with that prick," Liam said.

"I figured. But if I have to fly back out to Lake Tahoe to deal with his shit again anytime soon, we're gonna have to let his contract go. He harasses and verbally abuses everyone we send out; he won't keep himself out of the press, and he's about to lose his contract with his record label. With the rate he's going, he's gonna run out of funds soon too."

"I know."

I hated dealing with Jasper. I was just waiting for the final fuckup so we could officially be done with him.

"*Fuck*," I mumbled as I narrowed my eyes on Brittney's perfect little ass bent over Kayley's desk once again. Visions of fucking her bent over *my* desk flooded my brain.

This is going to be the cruelest form of torture.

"What?" Liam's voice snapped.

I cringed. Was I thirteen? It sure felt like it. I couldn't look at Brittney without focusing on sex. If she had any idea where my mind was every time she was near, she'd probably try to murder me. Although I still didn't get why she was so fucking mad.

"Nothing, I gotta go deal with something though. I'll catch up with you later."

We ended the call, and I watched Brittney, feeling like a dirty old perve. She shifted from foot to foot and pointed patiently to the computer screen, showing Kayley how to do something for what felt like the third time in an hour.

"Brittney?" I called a few minutes later as she walked by a small window that separated my office from a set of cubicles.

She stopped but didn't turn. Her back was ramrod straight and she pinched her eyes closed. It all screamed anguish. I hated that I made her feel that way. Finally, she pivoted, almost in slow motion, and entered through the door next to the window.

She took two small steps inside and did a quick scan of my office, starting with the sofa that sat next to the door, then the small table and chairs in one corner and the large windows behind me that looked out over Asheville. Finally, her eyes met mine.

"Yes?"

"What's with the twenty-year-old assistant with no experience?"

She laughed. "She's twenty-three. She has a college degree and some experience. She's just…"

"Helpless?" I'd dated enough of those women to know the type.

Brittney laughed that sexy-as-hell laugh again. I'd forgotten the way it made my body react. Luckily, I was sitting behind my desk and could adjust myself without her knowing how much she was already affecting me. This was going to be a long couple of months. Hopefully Hunter got his shit figured out quickly so I could get back to Nashville.

"Yep. Pretty much."

"Why are you the one helping her? Did you draw the short straw or something?"

She shrugged. "I'm the only one with the patience, and I did some of these things when I was interning here years ago. So, in a way, yeah; I drew the short straw." She glanced over her shoulder at Kayley's cubicle across from my open door. Making sure she couldn't hear us, I guessed. "Did you need anything?" She directed back at me.

I could think of a lot of things I *needed* from her, but none of them would be appropriate to say, so I shook my head and watched her hips sway as she walked out of my office.

I brought my hand to my mouth and bit down on my knuckle. I was her boss. We couldn't get involved. I could not fuck her again, no matter how badly I wanted to.

6

BRITTNEY

IT HAD BEEN a week since Derek had taken over for Hunter, and we'd fallen into a professional—aside from the times I caught him checking out my ass—routine. His perusal of my body was usually subtle, but I saw it on occasion. I may or may not have added a little extra sway to my hips when I noticed him staring. It served him right. I enjoyed showing him what he was missing.

I just wanted to go home and relax with a glass or two of wine and a smutty book. But instead, I was leaving work and going on a blind date. Why had I let Rachel talk me into this? Probably because I hoped I could meet someone who'd take my mind off the one guy I shouldn't want and could absolutely not have.

I stepped into the elevator and wanted to scream when Derek followed right behind me. Seriously, I couldn't catch a break. I jabbed the button for the lobby, ready to get the hell out of here.

"Bad day?"

"Nope. It was fine."

"So you always stab elevator buttons angrily?"

"Only when you're in the elevator."

He laughed. Like freaking laughed. He thought this was funny? I wanted to punch him.

Before I could lash out, the lights went out and the elevator jolted to a stop, causing me to stumble back in my heels. And right into a hard wall of muscle.

"Fuck," Derek mumbled as he gripped my upper arms. "You okay?" he asked close to my ear, sending a tremor straight to my core.

The emergency lights came on, and I stepped out of his grasp. I shook my head as he fished his phone from his pocket.

"No reception in here most of the time."

"Yeah, I'm not getting a signal."

I picked up the emergency phone and hit the red button to talk. After speaking with Bruce in security, we were advised to hang tight. They were working on getting the power back on, and he would call us back with an update.

Deciding I might as well get comfortable while I waited, I kicked off my shoes and sat on the floor with my back against the wall. Derek must not have felt the same way. He turned and braced one hand on the wall, bowing his head. Great, I'd probably have to deal with him sulking and complaining about being stuck here.

But he was quiet. He just stood there for the longest time, not moving, not saying a word, before he suddenly spun and sank to the floor, putting his forearms across his knees and his head down.

This was not the Derek I knew. He always had an air of self-confidence that bordered on cockiness. Now he almost seemed anxious and unsure.

"You alright?" I finally asked. The silence and his demeanor made me nervous.

I swallowed, my throat feeling dry when he didn't answer

right away. He took a deep breath and raised his gaze to meet mine.

"I'm a bit claustrophobic." He gave me a shy smile, and damn, was there anything about this guy I *didn't* find attractive? I mean other than how he'd snuck out in the middle of the night after giving me the best sex of my life? "It's Typically manageable. I avoid flying when I can, but I can get through it with a drink when I have to. Elevators are fine most of the time because the time I spend inside them is usually short. But this is utter hell right now."

"I'm sorry," I mumbled. "Is there anything I can do to help?"

The seductive smirk I'd seen multiple times appeared.

I shook my head. "Obviously you're fine."

He dropped his head back to his arms and murmured, "Talk to me."

"Huh?"

"Just talk. Help me get my mind off being stuck in an enclosed space with no way out."

I hesitated for a moment, unsure of what to say. But before I knew it, I found myself talking about a range of things. I told him about my time living in New York and asked about his life in Nashville. I talked about my hiking experience in Lake Tahoe, and somehow, almost twenty minutes had passed. I never talked about myself this much to anyone, ever. Not even Savannah.

"I'm glad you enjoyed it." He hesitated before continuing with, "You ready to tell me why you act like you hate me?"

I rolled my eyes. Was he serious? "I didn't appreciate being played and lied to."

"What the—" he stuttered, his brow furrowing for a moment before he spoke again. "I never lied, and I can't imagine how you think I played you."

I arched my eyebrows. "Did I imagine you telling me

you'd stay? I doubt it. But you snuck out in the middle of the night instead."

"I think we have a very different definition of staying over. We fell asleep with your head on my chest, which, for the record, is *not* typical of a one-night stand. I didn't realize you meant stay all fucking day." He took a deep breath and shook his head. "Come on, I never thought I'd see you again. I wasn't looking for anything serious, and I had an early flight to catch. I didn't want to wake you up at four a.m. and do the whole 'that was great,' awkward goodbye thing. I did exactly what I said I would."

The explanation was plausible, but it didn't make me feel much better. Maybe if I'd had more experience with one-night stands, I would have realized that, and maybe it wouldn't have hurt so much.

I shrugged. "Okay…" I hoped my cheeks weren't giving away the embarrassment I was feeling.

"Okay?"

"Yeah, what do you want me to say? I guess I'm naive and thought we shared something. I was hurt that you didn't feel the same."

"Fuck, I'm sorry, Brittney." We just stared at one another for a few agonizing moments before he said. "I did feel it though, for what it's worth."

"Feel what?"

"The connection. There's obviously something between us. There was that night, and there still is."

"Speak for yourself."

"Fine. I am."

We held eye contact for a beat, neither willing to break.

Finally, I caved, looking just over his shoulder—I felt less vulnerable this way—and saying, "Whatever, it doesn't matter now. You're my boss, and you're also not staying here, so it's best if we keep things between us strictly professional."

I glanced at my watch. I was almost forty-five minutes late to the blind date I didn't even want to go on.

"You had plans?" Derek asked.

"Yeah. A date."

The sound he made was like a mix between a growl and a huff. Was he jealous?

"Then I, for one, am happy we got stuck in the elevator."

"Well, that makes one of us."

I was actually glad to get out of the date, but I wasn't about to tell him that. I felt shitty about standing my date up without even a text to let him know I couldn't make it.

"I want to ask a question, but I don't want you to bite my head off. Can you manage that? I'm genuinely interested in knowing."

I wanted to say no, but instead, I sighed and acquiesced. "Go ahead."

"I'm assuming you have a law degree in order to step into Meredith's position."

"Correct."

"How old are you? You seem pretty young to have gone through college and law school already."

"I'm twenty-five. I graduated from high school at seventeen, then college at twenty-one. I finished law school when I was twenty-three. I've been here full time for about two years."

His eyes shone with admiration, and I could feel my cheeks heat.

"Most people don't take me seriously in this field. They think I'm young and useless, like Kayley. But I'm good at what I do."

"I can tell. You've impressed me on multiple occasions over the last week."

His eyes went dark as he watched me, but just as I opened my mouth to reply, the lights turned on and the elevator descended. It was like the universe was trying to remind us we couldn't go there.

Derek stood up and extended his hand. When I grabbed it, he pulled me to my feet, and the air shifted as he slowly backed me against the wall. I should have pushed him away. He gave me ample time to do so. We couldn't cross that line. But that invisible magnetic pull, the same one from that night in Lake Tahoe, was still there, and neither of us seemed able to resist it.

He braced both hands against the wall and pinned me with his heated stare. Our lips were inches apart. The air crackled between us. I wanted so desperately to feel his hands on me again.

Whether it was perfect timing or not, the elevator stopped, and the doors opened. He pushed off the wall and stepped back.

Once we stepped out of the building, Derek turned and focused those gorgeous green orbs on me. "Have a drink with me."

"Bad idea. We shouldn't go there." I wiped my clammy hands down the sides of my thighs.

"It's just a drink."

"We both know that's a lie."

His sexy as sin smirk caused a fluttering sensation in my stomach.

"See you tomorrow," I rushed, needing space before I changed my mind.

Turning, I started toward my apartment. I liked to walk to and from work if the weather was nice. I enjoyed the fresh air, and it saved on gas and parking.

"Let me at least walk you to your car." Derek came up beside me.

I raised one eyebrow at him. "I didn't drive."

He looked at me like I'd grown a second head, his head

cocked to the side and his brow furrowed in confusion. "I'll give you a ride then."

"No. I'm good, but thank you. I could use the fresh air."

He gave me another confused look but remained silent.

"Goodnight, Derek."

I turned and continued down the busy sidewalk, wondering how the hell I was going to do this. I'd almost let him kiss me in the elevator. In fact, I probably would have let him do so much more if we had been stuck in there any longer. And to be honest, if he had pushed a little harder, I might have given in and grabbed a drink with him, knowing full well where that would have led.

But I wanted more than he was willing to offer. I had to remember that. He'd repeatedly made it clear that he didn't want a serious relationship. And I didn't do casual. Besides, in a month or two, he'd be back in Nashville.

I just needed to keep my panties on until then.

7

DEREK

THE FIRM WAS SLAMMED with a high-profile case this week. I had to work directly with a young actress, her family, and their attorney to keep the press in the dark about the situation at hand.

Brittney's opinion on the case was invaluable. She had a public relations mind with legal training and pointed out things I didn't even see. And I finally convinced her to have lunch with me. Of course, it was a strictly working lunch to go over things for my meeting with the client later that afternoon, but getting her alone, even in a crowded restaurant to talk shop, excited me. Probably more than it should.

I couldn't look at my desk without breaking into a sweat and having to adjust my pants because last night I dreamed of her sitting on it, legs spread, while I used my tongue to make her scream my name. She monopolized my thoughts, and I wasn't sure if I loved it or hated it.

I glanced at my watch—almost noon. I stood, gathering my things, when Kayley walked into my office, wringing her hands and looking anywhere but at me.

"I'm sorry. I know you have a lunch meeting. But your

three o'clock called and said he needs to meet earlier. He said it's urgent, and he's on his way in."

Shit. That's not good.

"Okay, I'll get set up in the conference room. Can you bring him in when he gets here?"

"Oh. I—I have a nail appointment."

I locked my jaw. She was technically not my assistant, and unfortunately, Hunter hadn't given me the authority to fire her, so I gave her a brief nod and waited until she grabbed her stuff and headed for the elevator. I walked down to Brittney's office first, only to find it empty. Maybe she'd already left. I sent her a quick text letting her know I couldn't make it for lunch, then headed to the receptionist's desk to see if she would bring the client back for me. Ninety percent of the time, Sue, the receptionist, was more helpful and useful than Kayley anyway.

After my meeting, I worried about Brittney's wrath. She hadn't responded to my text, and my experience with women anytime I had to cancel plans due to work had never been positive. They either whined that I didn't make them a priority, or they were just pissed until I did something to make up for the broken plans. It was exhausting. My last serious relationship was the worst. She set the bar so unrealistically high that it didn't matter what I did. I could never do anything right.

But regardless of my experience, Brittney and I weren't dating, so she didn't have any reason to be pissed. Right? Clients came first. Surely, she knew that.

Fuck, I'm getting all worked up over a girl who isn't even mine.

I paused outside my office and spotted her walking down the corridor toward me with a takeout bag in her hand.

"I got you street noodles from the Thai place," she said, offering me the bag.

Well, this was a first. Not only did she not seem pissed,

but she also remembered what I liked from the Thai place we ordered from earlier in the week.

"You're not pissed?"

"Why would I be?" Her eyebrows pinched together as she tilted her head.

"'Cause I canceled our lunch da—plans."

Her cheeks heated like she'd caught on to what I'd almost said. "You had a meeting. Or was that a lie?"

A pair of mocha-colored eyes narrowed in my direction.

"Nope, I definitely had a meeting."

She studied me like she was trying to figure something out. "Anyone ever tell you that you're a bit strange?"

I laughed. "I've been called a lot of things. Never strange though."

"If you say so." She brushed past me, the scent of jasmine hitting my nose, sending visions of that night in Lake Tahoe swimming through my head. I wanted to pin her against the wall and hike her skirt up while my tongue explored her mouth. But I stood stock-still, afraid I'd do exactly that if I moved.

Brittney

DEREK WAS BEING SUPER WEIRD. I looked over my shoulder, noticing he still hadn't moved. He was like a statue, standing in the same position, holding his takeout bag.

Shaking my head, I turned on my heel and headed for my office. He could work things out on his own. I kicked my shoes off once inside my office and shut the door. I had a few hours of work left to do, and I didn't want to stay late.

It wasn't until a few people walked past my office, distracting me from the document I was studying on my computer, that I realized it had been more than three hours since I'd left Derek standing in the hall. I shut everything down, gathered my things, and headed toward the elevators but stopped outside of Derek's office when I heard him cuss to himself.

"Everything okay?" I asked, peering in. He was hunched over his laptop, his eyebrows scrunched up in frustration.

"No. Things just got more complicated with this high-profile client of mine, and now I might have to fly back out to Lake Tahoe for a difficult client I want to just let go. And of course, when I asked Kayley to look into flights, she couldn't figure out how to search for direct flights. I snapped at her and probably made the poor thing cry. Jesus, has she never booked a flight before?" He let out a deep breath.

"Let me help." I sat in the chair across the desk from him and pulled my laptop out. "When do you want to leave?"

"You don't have to do that—"

"I want to. And then you can pick my brain about the two clients."

An hour later, we had flights booked for *both* of us for next Monday and had talked about Jasper. I would be lying if I said I wasn't nervous. The last time we were *both* in Lake Tahoe, well—

But it was probably best if I went in case Derek really wanted to cut Jasper loose.

Now we were both working on damage control for the client who had come in earlier.

"Paparazzi are disgusting," Derek mumbled. "Look at this." He leaned back and pointed at the screen of his computer.

I walked around to his side of the desk and gasped at the image. I knew the original pictures leaked were of the

37

twenty-one-year-old actress and a thirty-year-old man coming out of a sex club. However, these pictures were detailed and painted a picture that, regardless of the truth, didn't look good. They would hurt her no matter how the media spun the photos.

"This ain't good. Either she gets labeled as a freak for enjoying kinky sex or as a victim of abuse."

He rubbed his eyes with the heels of his hands. "Yeah, and she's made it clear that she won't go the victim route. She told me in no uncertain terms that if it were up to her, she'd tell everyone she loves being spanked and having her hair pulled. Her family, though, is appalled and embarrassed. It was like an episode of Maury in there today. I think they need a family therapist, not a PR firm."

I laughed and leaned back against his desk. Our gazes locked, and when his heated look trailed down my body, I licked my lips and swallowed the ball of nerves lodged in my throat. I had kept my distance since being alone with him in the elevator, knowing I would cave if he touched me again.

"Derek…" I warned, glancing over my shoulder at the open door, but I stopped short when he stretched an arm out and brushed my leg just below the hem of my skirt.

He met my gaze again as his fingers slowly trailed under my skirt, hiking it up farther.

I shouldn't let it continue. Nothing good would come of it. But I was frozen, like my body just didn't give a shit about what my rational brain was trying to tell it.

"Tell me to stop," he growled as his thumb brushed ever so lightly over my panties. "If you don't want this, I need you to tell me. I don't want to fight it anymore."

I closed my eyes, relishing in the way a simple touch from him could make my body come alive.

"I—" A moan escaped through my parted lips as his thumb applied pressure.

"Words, Brittney. Tell me to stop or tell me you want this. I want to make you come on my hand. Is that what you want too?"

"Yes," I breathed. Desperate for his touch.

"Spread your legs for me."

I did as he instructed and planted my hands behind me on the desk for more support.

"Just like that." He moved my thong aside and slid two fingers along my slit.

My knees all but buckled when he finally sank them inside me, but I tensed, glancing over my shoulder at the open door when I remembered where we were.

"Britt, look at me." He moved his thumb slowly over my sensitive bud as he talked. "It's only us here, and I'm watching. Relax and focus on how I'm making you feel."

I nodded. And when he thrust his fingers in and out while circling my clit, I forgot all about where and who we were.

It didn't take long before pressure built in my core. I let out an involuntary moan, and when Derek's hand covered my mouth, I opened my eyes wide, locking them with his.

"Do you know how many fantasies I've had about you on this desk in the last two weeks?" He grinned and leaned closer, his eyes more black than green. "You sitting on it while I use my tongue to bring you pleasure. Bending you over it and sinking into your wet pussy. You on your knees under it, taking my hard cock into your pretty little mouth. So. Many. Fantasies."

The rough timbre of his voice skated across my skin as his dirty words sent me to the precipice. When he curled his fingers inside me, I tumbled over the edge and rode wave after wave of my orgasm until it finally subsided.

How, after one night together, did he know how to make my body respond like it did? How did he have so much control over me?

All I knew was my resolve to keep things strictly professional was crumbling.

And fast.

8

DEREK

I WAS DONE PRETENDING I didn't want this girl. I craved her in ways I hadn't truly experienced before now. She was smart, capable, independent, and sexy as fuck. I had no clue what would come of this, but I had no plans to leave her be.

Did that make me a selfish bastard? Probably.

I stood in front of her, placing my hands on the desk and caging her in.

"Go out with me," I said, holding her gaze, daring her to say no.

"Wh—what?"

"A real date."

She looked away, her signature tell—breaking eye contact. She was going to say no.

"We can't."

There it was. I stepped back and ran my hand through my hair.

"Have you ever just taken a chance on something?"

"Once. And I regretted it the next morning."

Ouch. That hurt. I mean, it shouldn't. She said she understood, but something told me she wouldn't settle for less than what she *needed* again. And I didn't want her to.

A weight settled in my gut as she walked around to the other side of the desk and gathered her things. I wanted to say something. Make promises I wasn't sure I could keep. She left my office like it was on fire, and once she was out of sight, I sank back down in my chair and threw my head back, staring at the ceiling.

I fought the urge to call Liam. With the stress of his brother's situation, the last thing I should do was burden him with my issues. I had a few months here. Maybe I could still convince her to give us a shot. We could figure out everything else. She deserved that, and she was worth the effort. For the first time in a long time, I *wanted* to put that type of effort into a woman.

THREE DAYS LATER, our company car pulled up in front of Brittney's apartment building. I got out to help her with her bag, and even though she thanked me sweetly, something was different. Like she had constructed a wall that hadn't been there before. But I liked a challenge. I just hoped it was one I could overcome.

"How was your weekend?" I asked, trying to cut through the overwhelming silence.

"Fine. Yours?"

"Fine." Her curt answer told me she had no interest in chatting, so I wouldn't push. Part of me wanted to call her out for acting her age, but instead, I watched her spend the next ten minutes angrily typing away on her phone and making the sexiest huffing noises.

"Everything okay?" I asked, nodding to her phone.

"No. Savannah grates on my last nerve. She thinks I should just agree to bang you while we're working together," she said with an eye roll. A slight redness spread up her neck, and she stared at her fingers as she picked at the nail polish.

I couldn't hide my smile at her rant, and when I glanced in the rear-view mirror at the driver, he raised his eyebrows. Obviously, he wasn't going to say anything.

At least I had Savannah in my corner. Maybe between the two of us, we could convince Brittney to give me a chance.

"I knew I liked her."

Brittney turned that heated glare on me, and as hard as I tried to stop it, I chuckled.

"I'm glad you think this is funny." She crossed her arms and turned to stare out the window.

"In my defense, I only asked for a date."

"Mm-hmm, okay."

I *had* only asked for a date, but she was right; that wasn't the only thing I wanted. I wanted her under me. I wanted her writhing from the things I could do to her.

We arrived at the airport, and I got my luggage, her luggage, and my carry-on bag and started for the entrance. I was abruptly yanked to a stop when Brittney grabbed her suitcase from me.

"I got it."

"You don't want me to wheel it in for you?"

"I appreciate the offer, but I'm capable of wheeling a suitcase myself."

I crowded her space, taking her by surprise as I lifted her chin with my knuckle.

"You are capable as fuck, and I find it extremely refreshing and sexy."

Her cheeks turned rosy, and fuck, if I wasn't careful, I was going to embarrass us in front of an airport full of people.

Once we were checked in and seated at our gate, she put a hand on my bouncing knee.

"You're not gonna lose it on the plane, are you?" she asked, her eyebrows drawn together in concern.

I looked at where her palm lay on my leg, how her fingers were splayed out, the contact from each one sending a current of electricity through me. Thoughts of her running it slowly up my thigh flooded me.

I smirked. "If I say yes, will you help distract me?"

She leaned forward, her mouth inches from my ear, and I had to clench my fists in order to keep my hands to myself.

"So, I take it you've never joined the mile high club?"

"Hell no. I'd consider it for you though." That was the truth. Sex in a tiny bathroom on a plane had never been appealing until her.

"You're not giving up, are you?"

Good. She understood how serious I was about what we could have.

"Nope." I immediately realized how that might have come off. "Unless you tell me you don't feel the same and want me to leave you alone. Then I will."

She looked away, and I said a silent prayer that she wouldn't utter those words.

9

BRITTNEY

IT DIDN'T TAKE LONG for me to get a firm grasp on this Jasper prick. He was one of those types who thought women should drop to their knees in front of him whenever he asked. During our meeting with him and his manager, he barely let me speak, interrupting me anytime I opened my mouth. The only time he acknowledged me was when I stood up or leaned over the table. But that was just to outright eye fuck me.

And then there was Derek. I was getting more and more worried that if we didn't get the hell out of this meeting, he was going to blow up and murder Jasper. Each time the jerk ogled me, Derek's jaw locked tighter.

"I don't know what your client wants from us," Derek directed to Jasper's manager.

"That one," Jasper said, nodding to me, "bent over in front of me might make up for your incompetence."

I didn't even have time to blink before Derek was on the other side of the table, gunning for Jasper. If his manager, Kevin, hadn't been between them, Jasper would've ended up with a bloody nose.

"We're done. *I'm done.* No one in the Nashville office will work with you. And frankly, coming out here to deal with your mess isn't worth the amount you pay us." With his hands balled into fists at his sides, Derek turned to Kevin. "Good luck finding him another PR team. We'll send over the termination forms tomorrow."

Once back in the rented car, I couldn't help but glance in Derek's direction. I had a brother who could be broody when he was pissed, so I should be used to this. But I didn't know what to make of Derek. He was usually so mellow.

"You know I've dealt with plenty of clients like Jasper, right? Men in this industry fail to take me seriously, but so do women. Because I'm young and female, people rarely consider that I might be smart and capable," I said as I relaxed against the leather seats, feeling the tension drain from my shoulders.

"That was different, and you know it. That was sexual harassment, and I'm ashamed to say it wasn't the first time. We should have gotten rid of him months ago."

I nodded. He didn't need me to tell him he was right.

"Want to go for a hike?" he said a few minutes later, turning in my direction. His face had lost all signs of anger. His jaw was no longer tight, and he wasn't white-knuckling the steering wheel any longer. The change in his mood and demeanor gave me whiplash. I'd never seen someone go from pissed off to chill in a matter of moments.

I smiled though, loving the idea. We didn't just share an amazing physical connection. I could see myself hiking the millions of trails around Half Moon Lake with him. My small hometown had breathtaking views. But that would never happen. I had to remind myself again that he wouldn't be staying in Asheville. Better to enjoy it in the here and now and not pine over what could never be.

"Sure. Want to show me another favorite spot?"

He grinned, and his eyes lit with something akin to a challenge. "Think you can handle a hard one? I'd love to show you Granite Lake and South Maggie's Peak."

"I had no problem handling the last hard one." Inspiration point hadn't been easy. I hoped I wasn't biting off more than I could chew with that statement.

"I'll give you something hard to handle," he mumbled, one side of his mouth turning up.

I took a moment to appreciate his body and felt, rather than saw, when his heated stare locked on me. I swiftly turned to look out my window, not making eye contact.

Two hours later, I *was* regretting my decision. Not really. But damn, were my legs burning. And Derek had been acting weird since we'd set off on the trail.

"We can turn back if you need to."

"Nope, I want to make it to the top." I wasn't giving up this far into it.

"That's my girl."

That comment caused me to stumble. Thankfully Derek was in front of me and hadn't witnessed it. Hearing him call me his girl did something strange to me.

He glanced back with his lips pressed together, like he too was thinking about the words he'd used. But then he glanced down, and his jaw locked. "Did you not bring actual clothes?"

"Wh—at?" I looked down at my athletic tank top and shorts.

"I can see your ass cheeks and most of your tits in that outfit." He kept his eyes averted and shook his head.

A hot flush crept up my neck. "Well, it's not like you haven't seen it all anyway."

He smirked. "Yes, I have. I do enjoy thinking about what you look like without clothes." He openly adjusted himself. "But having a constant hard-on while hiking isn't comfortable."

I rolled my eyes. "Your dramatics remind me of Savannah."

We stopped at the end of the trail, studying the breathtaking view of the lake. Strong hands gripped my hips, pulling me back against a hard chest—and something else hard that twitched against my ass cheeks. He wasn't joking earlier. Was he actually turned on by my sweaty hot mess in workout clothes?

I leaned back into him and rested my head on his shoulder, savoring this moment and wishing I could have it all.

"I want you. I know our situation isn't ideal, but I'm asking you to give whatever this is a chance for however long we have."

And there it was. The reminder that I couldn't, in fact, have it all. I could have what he was offering, but only until he went back to Nashville.

I wanted to say yes.

Would the reward be worth the risks?

"I'll think about it." I still wasn't sure if I could do a temporary, casual thing, and it would be unfair to ask for more. Wouldn't it?

He wrapped his arms around my waist, the heat of him seeping into me as we looked out over the lake. Standing there like that, feeling more at peace than I had in a long time, made my resolve crumble even more.

Derek

I SPENT the entire night in my hotel room tossing and turning. Damn, I had it bad for Brittney. And I didn't just want her body. Maybe we could try a long-distance thing for a bit, explore this connection. The more time I spent with her, the more I wanted us to be something real.

I kicked off the blankets, too worked up to sleep, and headed to the shower. Bracing one hand on the wall, I fisted my aching cock and closed my eyes. Images of Brittney on her knees flooded my mind. Her plump lips wrapped around my shaft, moving tortuously slow and taking all of me in. I grabbed her hair and set a punishing pace until I emptied into her mouth.

"*Fuck,*" I groaned as I came hard, pumping my cock dry.

Is she touching herself and thinking about me too? Fuck, I hope she is.

BETWEEN DRAFTING up the termination papers for Jasper and explaining what happened via a video conference with Liam, my morning flew by. After ending the call, I made my way to Brittney's room and knocked.

As the door swung open, I had to steady my hands on the adjacent wall. She was in nothing but a very skimpy, very short robe.

"Hey," I said, clearing my throat. "Do you want to grab dinner and drinks at The Silver Lining?"

"Uh—"

"I'm not asking for anything more than sharing good food and maybe a drink. Besides, it's trivia night. Could be fun."

She tilted her head at the words *trivia night.* Perfect. She was on the fence.

"Please?"

Wow, I'd resorted to begging now.

Yeah, real smooth. That's not desperate or anything. Fucking moron.

"Trying to use my love of rum runners and trivia against me, I see."

At the sight of her teasing smile, I wanted to fall to my knees and beg her for what scraps she'd be willing to give me. But I didn't. If she wanted to give us a chance, she'd have to decide that on her terms.

I shrugged. "Who doesn't love rum runners and trivia?"

"Alright, but I was just about to jump in the shower. Give me an hour?"

Shit. Now I would spend the next hour thinking of her naked and soapy in the shower.

Tonight's trivia theme was Marvel Cinematic Universe. Apparently, another random thing we shared in common was our love for all things Marvel. We kicked ass during the trivia competition, coming in second place to a group of guys decked out in Marvel T-shirts who were, if I was being honest, the stereotypical *Big Bang Theory* type nerds.

"That was so much fun. I need to find a place that does something like this in Asheville," Brittney said as she smiled like she'd just won the lottery.

She was competitive—a turn-on for me—and her enthusiasm over something like trivia was infectious.

"Yeah, that would be fun. Make it a weekly date."

Her eyes went round, and I fought back my gut reaction to backtrack. I wasn't going to apologize for telling her what I wanted. Instead, I was ready to lay it all out. I pulled my wallet from my back pocket and laid down the cash for the check, plus an extra dollar. I'd been to this bar a handful of times, and I'd seen plenty of people write wishes on dollar bills. I'd never done it before, but I'd never wanted to believe in magic until that moment.

Grabbing the pen from the table, I scribbled four words across the greenback and turned it around so she could see it.

"Just so we're clear about my intentions," I said.

She tried to hide it, but hope bloomed in my chest when a shy smile crossed her face.

I grabbed the dollar and gave Shawn a nod as I approached the end of the bar to tack my wish on the far wall. He sent me back a knowing smirk. She wasn't even my girl yet, and I was getting the *yeah, you're done for* look. If he only knew.

As I turned to make my way back to the table, I caught sight of a familiar couple standing behind the bar. I recognized Ryan Daily, who played baseball for the Metros immediately, but it took a second to place the woman with warm skin and dark, curly hair. It finally clicked; Bridget was one of the owners of the Silver Lining that I'd met on a previous visit to Lake Tahoe.

"Hey, Ryan," I said as I leaned against the bar top.

"Yeah, man?" Ryan cocked one eyebrow, eyeing me with the look that said *I'm friendly until you annoy me.*

"Are the rumors true? You getting traded?"

"I don't know, we'll see." He shrugged.

I tracked his subtle movement as he placed his hand on Bridget's belly. Interesting.

"Ryan," Bridget said as she gently swatted his shoulder. "If we're not telling everyone yet, then stop making it so obvious."

"Congratulations, you two." I kept my voice low. There was nothing in the media, as far as I could remember, about Ryan becoming a father. So they must have been doing a good job keeping it away from the press. Reporters would get wind of it eventually though. They always did.

"Thanks," Bridget said as she tilted her head slightly. "Don't tell me you're back here dealing with Jasper again."

"Afraid so, but we just cut ties. I'll miss coming to the bar, but I can't say I'll miss having to come out here to deal with him."

"Understandable."

I let my gaze wander back to Brittney. She placed her phone down on the table and looked up. A smile lit up her face as she held eye contact with me, and I prayed I was right about the desire stamped on her face.

"If you'll excuse me, I have a girl to win over."

10

BRITTNEY

HE'D WRITTEN *WISHING to be yours* on a dollar bill and put it on the wall. What was I supposed to do with that information? I wanted that too, but how? He'd eventually leave, and I'd stay in Asheville, near my family, and we'd never speak again. What else could happen? We'd become one of many failed long-distance relationships? And if one of us was able to transfer locations, how would that work? After how I witnessed Meredith and Hunter's situation play out, a romantic relationship with a coworker seemed like a bad idea. Plus, he didn't want more than casual. He'd told me that the night I met him.

And now I'd just come full circle with my thoughts. Was he wishing to be mine for a night? A week? A month? Or in a more permanent way? If I were Savannah, I would demand answers. Oh, who was I kidding? She wouldn't want to know the answers anyway. She would live in the moment or whatever.

My phone dinged with a response from Savannah. I had sent her a text when Derek walked to the bar.

Savannah: Oh lord, put the poor guy out of his misery and fuck him already. STOP over thinking and just live in the moment for once. Be me.

Yup, exactly what I'd just said to myself. Maybe she was right. Would I regret not taking the chance to have whatever this could be with him? Even if it ended when he went home?

"Do you want to take a walk along the water before we head back to the hotel?" Derek's question startled me from my thoughts as he sat down at the table.

"Sure." This would give me more time to think.

The silence that fell between us as we walked along the beach helped clear my head. I wanted to be free of worry like Savannah and take this chance.

We came upon a small cluster of rocks that jutted out into the water. I followed Derek as he climbed up and then turned around to give me a hand.

Once we'd found a flat spot to sit, Derek finally broke the silence. "If you want me to back off, I will."

I looked out over the water, searching for the right way to respond. I did *not* want that. I turned and studied him. The sky was newly darkened, but his face shone in the lights from the restaurant down the beach. I gave a slight shake of my head before he reached out and tucked one piece of hair behind my ear. My eyes locked on his lips, and I wished he would kiss me. The passion of our first night together had been alcohol induced. The other day in his office had been a heat-of-the-moment experience. Now, though, I was consciously choosing to be with him, even if it was tempo-rary. As if he could read my mind, he slid his hand to the back of my head and pulled me closer.

His lips moved softly against mine. He didn't rush to deepen the kiss. Instead, he let me savor every stroke. My whole body came alive, like a ripple from a wave, and when I leaned into him with a moan, his tongue surged inside. In the next second, he was pulling me onto his lap. The slow, sensual kiss became desperate as I straddled him. I moved then, searching for the friction I so desperately needed.

When his hands slid under my sweatshirt and the cold air hit my back, I sucked in a breath. My movements slowed; our breaths white puffs of air between us as the evening air cooled by the minute.

"We should head back," he whispered before he pressed his warm lips against my forehead.

I nodded but didn't want to break this moment. Reluctantly, I climbed off his lap, and we made our way back to the car. I couldn't help smiling when he grabbed my hand.

The whole way back to the hotel, I hoped that the night would end with us finishing what we'd just started.

11

DEREK

ALL I WANTED WAS to spend the entire night naked, tangled with Brittney. But I was second-guessing crossing that threshold. I wanted her to trust me. To trust this, us. She needed to know this wasn't a one-time thing for me.

All rational thought left me when she reached over the middle console and palmed my cock through my pants. I groaned, closed my eyes, and gritted my teeth. Between her rocking against me back on the shore and now the way she was stroking me, I was pretty sure there was no blood left in my head.

I grabbed her hand, intertwining our fingers, and rested them on my thigh. "You gotta stop, or I'm going to embarrass myself."

She chuckled, and that sexy little sound did nothing to get my blood flowing above the belt. I couldn't help but smile as I thought about how she would react if I brought her close to the edge of an orgasm, stopped, and started all over again. She was so responsive, her facial expressions and the noises she made showing exactly what she was feeling. I knew she struggled to get out of her head. I wanted to spend hours worshipping her body and discovering all the ways I could help her focus on her own pleasure. I got the impression from our first night together that she had never had an attentive partner before me, and I was ready and willing to show her just how studious I could be.

Once we stepped into the elevator alone and the doors closed, I pinned her against the wall and molded my mouth to hers, swallowing her gasp. When the doors opened on our floor, I grabbed her by the hand and pulled her down the corridor.

Her eyes were wide as I pushed her against the wall outside of my room, placing my hands above her head and leaning down so our faces were only a breath apart.

"This wouldn't be a one-night thing. So be sure before you come in."

She looked down, breaking eye contact before slowly nodding. "Okay."

With one finger, I lifted her chin and searched for the answer I was seeking. I wanted all of her; did she understand that?

"Okay, you're sure? Or okay, you understand it wouldn't be a one-time thing?"

"Both. I'm sure, and I want more than one night too."

That was all I needed to hear.

I pushed off the wall and pulled the key card from my pocket. The door wasn't even shut behind me before she was removing her sweatshirt. I followed suit, unzipping and discarding my lightweight jacket.

We did this dance back and forth, each of us removing an article of clothing and drinking the other in. I let it go until she was standing there in a matching bra and panty set.

I need to touch her.

I wanted more. Not just physically, but more of everything.

I moved quickly, grabbing her by the hips and spinning her so her ass pressed back against my straining cock.

My dick twitched against her, and I groaned, torn between wanting to take my time and needing to be buried inside her.

I trailed my mouth from her jaw down her neck, tasting the sweetness of her skin before dipping my hand under her panties.

My fingers were slick as they slid through her soaking wet pussy. "So ready for me."

She nodded and moved her hips, wiggling her ass against me, demanding more. After I pushed two fingers inside, she was riding my hand within seconds.

I was dying to taste her, and I didn't want her to come just yet.

She let out the cutest little whine when I stopped and pulled my fingers out.

"Not yet, sweetheart." I unsnapped and removed her bra, giving each of her hard nipples a pinch and loving the desperate moan she gave me in return. Inch by agonizing inch, I pulled her thong down the legs I wanted wrapped tightly around me. The feel of her silky skin kicked my need for her up a notch. I grabbed a foil packet from my wallet and discarded my boxers before rolling a condom on. "Put your hands on the bed and spread your legs," I said as I applied light pressure to her back, leading her to bend forward.

Damn, I could keep her like this forever.

Dropping to my knees, I went to work with my tongue, licking and sucking on her clit until her movements and sounds had me impatient to be inside her.

Her frustrated groan as I stood was followed by a gasp when I flipped her onto the edge of the bed and entered her in one swift movement.

"Oh god, Derek," she screamed.

I didn't pause, didn't hesitate, but continued to thrust, watching her facial expressions and letting the noises she made guide me. Her orgasm came fast and hard. Her walls spasmed around me as I gritted my teeth to hold back my own release.

"That's it, Brittney. Come all over my cock." The fantasies I'd had of this moment were nothing compared to the feel of her tight pussy gripping me like a vise as I continued to pump in and out of her. Within minutes, she was on the verge of another orgasm. "Fuck, you feel so good. Got another one for me?"

She thrashed her head from side to side with a moan as I found her sensitive nub and pressed hard, moving my thumb in circles. I was too close. I needed her to come again.

"Britt—" I groaned.

Her eyes popped open and locked on to mine as she tightened around me again. I slammed into her twice more, then followed her over the edge.

Continuing to brace myself above her, I brushed my lips against hers. The way she looked at me with hooded eyes and parted lips when she came mesmerized me. It was like she had never experienced anything like that before. To be honest, I hadn't either. Her fingernails still digging into my ass and the way she sucked on my bottom lip made me hard again in anticipation of round two.

"I need to take care of the condom," I murmured, pulling out of her wet heat and eliciting another moan from her.

When I came back to the bed, she was asleep. She barely stirred as I climbed in next to her and pulled her into my side. All that gorgeous hair falling across my chest had my muscles clenching once more. I lay there staring at the ceiling, running my fingers through her silky locks.

It should have scared me how important she had become, but I had no intention of walking away from her.

BRITTNEY

I WOKE up draped along Derek's side, my head resting on his chest and our legs entangled. Cuddled into him, I listened to the slow rhythm of his breathing. I pressed my lips against his hard pec and smiled when his muscles twitched.

I'd never experienced a connection like that with someone. Every touch, every kiss set my skin on fire, awakening parts of me I never knew existed. And I wanted more.

I traced the outlines of his abs as I trailed one finger down to his erection and wrapped my fist around it.

A sharp intake of air came from above my head, and I glanced up to watch his expression. His eyes blazed as he looked at me, like he was hungry and hadn't eaten in days.

This time was slow and sensual. I teased every inch of his body with my hands and my mouth, loving the control he let me have to explore. But when he flipped me and gave me the same slow exploration, I thought I was going to die if he didn't enter me.

"Derek. I need you. Please," I begged as he grabbed another condom and rolled it on.

He braced himself above me, tenderly brushing the hair away from my face before his warm lips caressed mine.

Then he made love to me. It was so different from the night before, but it felt just as incredible. He entered me inch by inch and brought me to orgasm with slow, purposeful movements before giving in to his own release.

"That was—" I started, searching for the words to describe how he made me feel. We were still naked and cuddled together. My head was on his chest as I ran one finger in circles around his stomach.

"Amazing? Out of this world? Indescribable?"

I chuckled. Good to know I wasn't the only one who felt it.

"Yes. All of that." I bit the inside of my lip. "At least I know you'll be here in the morning."

It was meant as a joke. But when he gently rolled me onto my back and narrowed his eyes as he hovered above me, I knew he didn't think it was funny.

"Brittney, I'm not going anywhere. You hear me? I need you to trust me."

I nodded. "I do."

Even though he wouldn't just walk away without a word this time, the bottom line was that he *was* going to walk away. Sure, it wouldn't be a one-time thing. We'd have more nights like this back home, but soon it would have to end. When the time came, he would go back to Nashville, and my life would continue on in Asheville.

I knew in that moment, no matter how hard I tried, I would be devastated when it was over. It was what I was afraid of. Giving in to my feelings and then knowing how much it would hurt when he walked away.

13

BRITTNEY

THE NEXT WEEK WAS HECTIC. We spent office hours working on the young actress's case, trying to retract the pictures and information that had been leaked. The more we tried, the more we worried there wasn't a way to fix it all. With each solution we proposed, the client and her family were at odds with how to approach it. Time was ticking, but no amount of explaining helped get them on the same page. I wanted to pull the client aside and tell her to do what was best for her career and ignore her family. Because that was what it boiled down to—her career. But I understood her need to not disappoint the people who loved and supported her.

Derek and I spent almost every night together. We went out to dinner, caught a movie one night, and even played mini golf over the weekend. After each date, we would inevitably end up at one of our places, desperate for each other.

We didn't really talk about what was going to happen once he went back to Nashville. He wanted to enjoy the here and now. I knew that based on the conversation we'd had when we first met. And I was trying to do the same, even though, deep down, I wanted to put a plan together. I wanted to know what our next move would be. Walking away when this was over would be the hardest thing I'd ever do, and that became more clear with each day we spent together.

Or maybe it didn't have to be over. Could he stay instead of going back to Nashville? Would he? I didn't know if he even wanted more than temporary, but I didn't ask. If the answer was no, I wasn't ready to hear it. The lack of a plan was driving me insane. Since I was a kid, I'd had my entire life planned out. I worked hard in high school to go to the college I wanted. I busted my ass in college and continued on to law school like I planned. I *always* had a plan.

I glanced down at our hands, Derek's wrapped firmly around mine, as we walked to the small pub for trivia night. Savannah was meeting us. She was casually hooking up with some guy who lived here in the city, but her response to my "you should bring him" was "ew, no. Why would I do that?"

This guy was good enough to have sex with, but not to bring to trivia night? I did *not* understand that girl.

As the three of us nursed our drinks after coming in third place, I told her about our client and the struggles we were having.

I ignored Derek's raised eyebrows at me and finally waved him off. "She's cool. She went to school for this crap, and she gives good advice. I've been trying to talk her into coming to work for Hunter."

"Yeah, no, I'm good. He seems like a waste of space."

Derek choked on a mouthful of beer at Savannah's words.

She raised her eyebrows at us. "Tell me I'm wrong."

"You're not," we said in unison.

I went on to explain how we weren't seeing a way to rectify the situation with the client.

"Look, you can't get blood from a stone," Savannah interjected. "Accept that this one isn't fixable."

I rolled my eyes as Derek said, "What?"

Savannah chuckled. "Honestly, I want to high five your client and tell her I like kink too. Especially—"

"Please don't finish that sentence," I said with a cringe.

"What I'm *trying* to say is just release a statement that her private life is just that—private—and what she does behind closed doors is no one's business. Then spend the next six months getting positive media coverage. Get the couple to volunteer with your brother's cancer kids. Everyone loves kids with cancer."

My eyebrows rose to my hairline. "Savannah," I scolded.

"What? It's true. Play on emotions. Show them visiting sick kids and orphaned puppies or whatever."

"She's right." Derek finally spoke up. "There is no perfect solution. We need to get the client and her family to see that this is the *only* solution."

"Of course I'm right," Savannah said with a shrug. "And maybe suggest she keep her blinds closed from now on."

We all chuckled and raised our glasses to that.

"And why aren't you doing this again? You should come to Nashville and work for me."

My breath caught in my throat. There was the answer to my biggest question. He still planned to go back to Nashville. So what did that mean for us? He'd told me before that he wasn't looking for anything serious.

I looked away, refusing to see the scrutiny or pity in Savannah's eyes. I wasn't sure if Derek sensed my need to pull away or what, but he wrapped an arm around my shoulders and tucked me into his side.

When we started this a little over a week ago, I'd decided I would try my best to live in the moment. But who was I kidding? This wasn't me, and I started to doubt if I could handle any of it.

Savannah cleared her throat. "I'm good. I have a job."

I laughed. "You're a part-time bartender at your family's restaurant and work for your brother, who you complain about daily."

She shrugged. "He's an idiot, but part-time bartender works for me. I'm still finding myself and have no interest in a nine to five."

Derek glanced at me with one eyebrow raised. I was used to Savannah's unwillingness to be tied down to anything or anyone. She was the textbook definition of free spirit, and I wasn't sure anything would tame her.

An hour later, Derek and I walked down the busy city street again. Maybe it was just in my head, but the silence was deafening. He hadn't corrected what he'd said earlier or even used it as a catalyst to figure out our next move. I'd gone into this knowing full well that our time together would be temporary. He needed to go back to his life in Nashville when his work here was done. So why did it bother me so much to hear him confirm it? I wanted to enjoy what we had and not stress over it. I'd have to try harder and prepare myself to walk away when it was time.

I could *not* fall in love with him.

14

DEREK

Was there such a thing as a professional hard-on? Not only was Brittney sexy as hell no matter what she was doing, but watching her handle a politician, one of our biggest clients, left me with a semi all afternoon.

She was in her element. And fuck, was she good.

I adjusted myself again for what felt like the tenth time in the last twenty minutes. I wanted to throw her across my desk and slam into her until she was screaming for release.

After witnessing Brittney kick ass this morning, I knew what needed to happen so we could continue our relationship. Because what the meeting cemented for me was that she wouldn't be happy in Nashville. We had a strong legal team. Working with well-known musicians meant we had to. Brittney would have to take a back seat to the more seasoned members of our legal team if she transferred there. So, the only choice, other than doing some stupid long-distance thing that I had no interest in, was for me to transfer here.

Our Nashville office was larger in volume of clients and revenue. Liam needed me. Maybe I could work for Liam remotely. At least until he found someone else. Frankly,

Bryan could fill my shoes there; according to Liam, he had been doing a good job over the last month.

As if my thoughts conjured the little temptress herself, Brittney stepped into my office with a smile.

"I have all the papers drawn up from this morning," she said as she approached my desk.

"Thank you." I stood and walked around her, peeking out into the hallway and finding it empty. Kayley was out sick, and most everyone else had already left. The office was a ghost town on Friday afternoons. It wouldn't have mattered if the whole team was standing outside my office. I needed her more than my next breath.

I shut the door and engaged the lock, then turned back to face her. When she placed her hands on her hips and shook her head, I shot her a smirk. Neither of us broke eye contact, though, as I stalked toward her, backing her into my desk.

I rested a hand at the nape of her neck and used my thumb to tilt her head back while I pressed my aching cock into her hip.

"I've had this problem since about ten o'clock this morning." Thrusting my hips, I made sure she knew what I was talking about. "Ever since I watched you handle that meeting like a fucking badass."

She made a sound that was somewhere between a contented sigh and a moan. Like she was as desperate as I'd been for the last three hours.

"Derek, we ca—" I cut her off as I devoured her mouth. Her gasp of surprise gave me the opening I needed to thrust my tongue inside and work her into a frenzy.

I trailed my lips to her ear, biting and licking until she reached for my belt.

I spun her and bent her over the desk before hiking her skirt up around her waist and yanking her panties down.

"Fuck," I hissed once I had the condom on and was

entering her inch by glorious inch. She felt so good, and once I was buried to the hilt, I leaned forward, kissing and sucking on her neck.

"Derek," she whispered.

"What do you need?"

"Move. Please."

I chuckled. I needed that too. For every thrust I made, she pushed back into me. I was so close already, since I'd spent the last three hours fantasizing about this. I reached around and fingered her clit fast and hard while my other hand covered her mouth to muffle her moans.

We came together as I continued to pump inside her, her tight pussy milking me dry.

I collapsed across her back, wanting to undress her and throw her on the couch and do that all over again. But we both still had work to do. So, it would have to wait until tonight.

After we cleaned up and made ourselves mostly presentable—the first two buttons of her blouse were undone, just the way I wanted them—I sat in my desk chair and pulled her onto my lap. I claimed her mouth once again and brushed my lips along her neck, breathing in hints of jasmine and sex.

She sighed and started to wiggle away from me. "I gotta get back to work."

"But I want to sit here and make out like teenagers," I mumbled against the top of her exposed breasts.

She giggled. "Me too, but I have to get a few more things done before five."

"Fine." Reluctantly, I let her get up. "Dinner?"

"Sure, sounds good."

I smiled as I watched her inch the door open, peek out, and then step out into the corridor.

After a moment, I picked up the phone and dialed Liam.

He answered after the second ring. "Ready to come home?"

I chuckled. "It's actually why I was calling."

"That bad?"

"No, no. The opposite. Wanted to see what you thought about the possibility of me staying on here," I hedged. I'd feel him out before spilling everything.

But the silence from the other end of the line worried me. "Uh—"

"No need to make a decision just yet, but if you wanted to talk it over with Hunter, I'd love the opportunity."

"Okay. I'll mention it to him. So, you're enjoying it there?"

"Yeah, man."

"It's a slower pace, I bet. I forget sometimes the extra hours we put in here."

"It's not just that. But we can talk more about my reasons once I know if it's even an option."

"Okay, I'll get back to you soon. It sounds like Hunter and Meredith should be finalizing their agreements shortly."

I swallowed over the lump in my throat. Damn, I thought I had more time to figure out how to make things work with Brittney.

But it didn't matter if it was tomorrow or a month from now. I did *not* want to go back to Nashville.

15

BRITTNEY

I'D HAD brunch with Meredith over the weekend, and I couldn't get our conversation out of my head. Hearing her say she'd accepted a job offer in New York and that the divorce settlements were being finalized over the next week had my stomach in knots. Once that happened, there would be no reason for Hunter to stay away. And Derek would need to go back to Nashville.

The thought of him leaving made me miserable. I had done the one thing I'd been telling myself not to. I'd fallen in love with him. But I couldn't tell him that. He loved his life in Nashville, and I wouldn't let him stay here or force some long-distance thing out of guilt or obligation. I had known what I was getting into. And I'd known in Lake Tahoe that my feelings went deeper than just physical.

I took a deep breath and tried to focus on work. But my mind was whirling. Should I end things now? Would that be easier than waiting for him to tell me he was leaving?

Oh my god, would he even tell me? Or would he just leave?

He asked me to trust him; he wouldn't do that again. Right?

Rachel stepped into my office, and the way her face fell caused me to pinch my eyes closed. She shut the door and plopped down into one of the chairs across from me.

"You look like shit."

"Thanks."

"What's wrong? Trouble in paradise?"

I had confided in her shortly after my second trip to Lake Tahoe. She had warned me then to tread lightly—I wasn't Savannah. She had always been the angel on one shoulder while Savannah was the devil on the other. Savannah pushed me outside of my comfort level, and Rachel was good at reminding me of my limits.

"He's probably leaving in the next week or so. Meredith said things are almost wrapped up."

"Oh?" She tilted her head and narrowed her eyes. "You're in love with him, aren't you?"

I couldn't say it out loud. It would make it too real.

"It doesn't matter. He's leaving."

"Have you asked him if that's what he wants?"

"He offered Savannah a job with him at the Nashville office at trivia night last week." She opened her mouth, probably to argue with me, but I held up my hand. "I knew what I was getting into. It's my fault, and it is what it is. I'll be fine."

She shook her head and hesitated before saying, "If you say so."

I was a coward, but I needed space and time to pull myself together, so I left early when I knew Derek was tied up in a meeting. When I got home, I ignored his phone calls and texted to tell him I wasn't feeling well. It wasn't a lie. My head was pounding, and my stomach would not settle.

I was curled up on the couch with a hot cup of tea and a romance novel, tearing up at the end, when everything would be tied up into a pretty little bow, and the main characters would ride off into the sunset together to live happily ever after. Real life wasn't like that. I was jealous of fictional characters. What had my life come to? I was almost thankful for the buzzing of the door.

That was until I pushed the button for the intercom and Derek's voice came through.

What the hell was he doing here?

Derek

WHEN BRITTNEY OPENED HER DOOR, my worry for her shot up. Her skin was pale, and the usual brightness in her eyes was missing.

"Oh, baby, you don't look so good."

"Um, thanks?"

I chuckled and stepped into her apartment. "You know what I mean." I placed my hand on her lower back and guided her to the couch that acted as a divider between the open concept living and dining rooms. I wanted to take care of her, and I needed her to see that. To see that I wanted to be here. Do all the little things. "I brought you wonton soup from the Chinese place you like."

She widened her eyes slightly before she shook her head. "You didn't have to do that. And you probably shouldn't be here. I might get you sick."

"Eh, that's okay. Then we can skip work together and stay curled up in bed."

She pinched her eyes closed like she was in pain. I should get her something for her headache. She felt a little warm too. "Where's your ibuprofen? You should eat and then take two."

She nodded and pointed down the hallway toward where the bedrooms and bathroom were. "Medicine cabinet in the bathroom."

After I got her situated, I grabbed the pills and came back to find her staring into her soup.

"Is it okay?" Worry crept up my spine. She was definitely not herself.

"Huh?"

"The soup. Is it okay?" I asked again as I handed her the two tablets in my hand.

"Oh. Yes, it's good. Thank you."

I sat down next to her on the couch. "How about I put an Avengers movie on while you eat? Then I can hold you for the rest of the night."

She nodded again and went back to staring at her soup while I put the movie on.

An hour later, she was asleep in my arms. I carried her to her bed and lay next to her. My dick twitched when I pulled her ass back against it.

Calm the fuck down, dude. That's not happening tonight.

I'd only been in two serious relationships before Brittney, and I'd dreaded having to wait on those women hand and foot. It had been exhausting catering to their every need, but with Brittney, it felt right. She was so capable and independent that when I had the opportunity to take care of her, it filled me with joy.

Was this what love was? Was I in love with her?

DEREK

BRITTNEY SEEMED to bounce back quickly, and maybe it was all in my head, but she had seemed more distant since I'd stayed with her a couple of nights ago.

Hunter would be back next week, and Liam had called to ask if I could spend the week getting him caught up. He didn't mention my request, and I didn't want to tell Brittney until I knew it was confirmed. Hunter had been running this firm pretty much by himself for a while, so he could say no. I had no clue how to broach the subject with Brittney without getting her hopes up.

I needed to see her though. I wanted to ask her to travel to Boston with me to visit some of my family for Thanksgiving. My dad was no longer with us, so it was just my mom and some extended family.

I stepped into her office and took a seat across from her.

She looked up, tilting her head. "Did you need something?" she said with a little bite to her tone.

I swallowed over the thickness in my throat, racking my brain. Why was she angry with me?

"What are your plans for Thanksgiving?"

"Oh. Um, I'm having my brother and my parents over. My mom had back surgery last month, so I figure this way she won't feel the need to do too much." Pausing, she stared at her fingers as she picked at the polish. Was she nervous about having me meet her family, or was that moving too fast for her? "I heard Hunter will be back next week." She lifted her head, questions swimming in her eyes.

Shit, I was hoping for more time to address this. I ran my hand through my hair, gathering my thoughts.

"Yeah, I'll spend next week catching him up on every-thing, and then I was thinking about going back home to Boston to visit my family the following week for Thanksgiv-ing. Maybe you cou—"

She cut me off. "Derek, look—" She glanced away. Some-thing was definitely wrong. She rarely broke eye contact; it was one of the things I loved about her. And when she raised her gaze back to meet mine, it was like she was staring right through me. "We don't have to do this. Or make this awkward. We agreed that this would be casual."

Wait, what? When did we agree this would be casual? What the fuck was she talking about? I clenched my jaw because I didn't trust myself to speak quite yet. I thought I was clear in Lake Tahoe that this wouldn't be a temporary thing. That I wanted more.

"What are you saying?" I needed to hear the words. Needed her to tell me she didn't want that now.

"I'm saying let's not drag this out. Let's just end things now."

This couldn't be happening. The one woman I had actu-ally fallen for and could see a future with didn't feel the same.

I didn't regret the time we'd spent together. And I wouldn't make this harder for her. I hated when people tried to force relationships when one person wasn't one hundred percent in. I wanted her to want this, not feel obligated.

Fuck. Who was I? I just wanted her happy, even though there was an ache in my chest I'd never experienced before. I guess it served me right. I was thirty and had never experienced a broken heart until now. I'd dated other women, broken their hearts, but never let myself care enough to feel this way. Fucking karma.

I nodded and stood, resigned. "If that's what you think is best. I'll let Liam know I'll be back as soon as I get Hunter caught up." I turned and stalked out of the door. Once in my own office, I threw myself into work.

Anything to get my mind off Brittney.

Brittney

IF THAT'S what I think is best?

What the hell was that supposed to mean? What did *he* think was best? To continue this until the minute he had to go? To hook up whenever he was in town? What did he want from me?

Whatever. He hadn't corrected me when I reminded him that he'd only wanted casual, so that confirmed what I already knew. And it was best this way. I couldn't keep doing this knowing how I felt about him. It was totally my fault too. He warned me, and I let myself fall anyway. A small part of me had hoped I was wrong, though, after he came to check on me and took care of me Monday night.

It felt weird leaving for the day, knowing we weren't going out and that I wouldn't feel his lips again. Or his body against mine. I would probably sleep like crap tonight. I had gotten used to falling asleep in his arms after our lovemaking. No. Sex, not lovemaking. It might have been love for me, but it was just sex for him.

I paused outside his office and stared at his closed door. The urge to knock and beg him to ignore everything I said and fuck me one last time was strong. But I made my feet move, faster and faster, until I was out on the city sidewalk.

A pint of ice cream and maybe a horror movie where no one lived happily ever after would cheer me up. Maybe.

17

DEREK

THE LAST WEEK had been utter hell. Every time I saw Brittney, I wanted to drop to my knees and beg her to be with me. Once I was back in Nashville, I wouldn't be reminded of her all the time. I just needed to get through the next few days.

Hunter came into the office twice and barely paid attention to anything I said. His mind seemed to be elsewhere still. I thought he was coming back because everything was resolved.

I was alone with my thoughts, sitting in my office, when my phone rang. Glancing at the screen, I swiped to answer when Liam's name popped up.

"I have really good news," he said before I could even say hello.

"Okay," I mumbled.

"Hunter wants to take a permanent step back. He says he's burned out. So we want to offer you the position there."

Fuck me.

"Oh."

"You… are you alright? You don't sound excited. If

you're thinking of going somewhere else, we can match whatever they're offering. I refuse to lose you to another firm."

"I—" Now I felt like a real piece of work. He thought I was fishing for a promotion or a raise. "Nah, man. That's not it. Things didn't quite work out here the way I hoped, and now I'm not sure I want to stay."

An exasperated huff came through the line. "I'm lost. You wanted the position and now you don't?"

"It's, um, more complicated than that." How much should I tell him? I was her boss, and he was mine. But I needed to tell someone. "I met someone."

He laughed. "That makes sense. It's always a fucking woman. They make men crazy."

Ain't that the truth.

When he didn't continue, I realized he was waiting for me to elaborate. I ran my hand through my hair and blew out a breath. "It's Brittney. In legal."

"Jesus Christ, what the hell is going on down there? Is there something in the water?"

"Haha, fuck you." The similarities between my situation with Brittney and Hunter and Meredith were ironic. But it ended there. If I had Brittney, I would do whatever it took to keep her.

"So, what happened?"

That's a good question.

I told him everything. When we hooked up in Lake Tahoe the first time and my disappearing act. How we reconnected the second time we went to Lake Tahoe.

"Is that why you took her with you?"

"Nah, man, it wasn't like that. It was her idea to go with me because of the situation with Jasper."

"So what's the problem?"

"She doesn't feel the same. She said she wanted to end

things rather than drag them on. That we agreed this was just gonna be casual. But I never agreed to that."

"Did you tell her that? You explained how you felt about her and told her you planned to stay so you guys could be together, right?"

He said it like he had faith I wasn't an idiot. I needed him to understand though.

"No. I didn't want her to feel guilty about trying to end things. No use spewing my feelings on her like a lovesick puppy."

There was a pause and then, "Jesus Christ. Women aren't going to tell you exactly how they feel. They're like Rubix Cubes with no matching colors, and you just gotta do the best you can to figure them out. Don't you think I get in trouble with the old lady all the time?" When I didn't say anything, he added, "Trust your gut. You have one of those weird abilities to read a room. What did your gut tell you about how Brittney felt about you?"

"I thought she felt the same. The way she looked at me made me…" I was convinced she was falling in love with me too. Had I read her wrong?

"Go get your girl, dumbass."

"What if she doesn't want more?"

"Then you come home knowing you tried. Sometimes the one is worth fighting for."

Was he right? Was Brittney the one for me? And here I was, letting her slip through my fingers. I hung up with Liam and marched down to Brittney's office, determined to tell her how I felt about her.

My determination crumbled when I found her office empty. I turned and headed down the corridor.

"Hey, any idea where Brittney is?" I asked, poking my head into Rachel's office.

She looked up and narrowed her eyes. "Even if I did, I

wouldn't tell you. I warned her not to trust you, that you would only hurt her."

What. The. Fuck? I couldn't believe—wait, if Rachel thought Brittney could get hurt in this, then that had to mean Brittney wanted more. Otherwise, Rachel wouldn't be looking at me like she wanted to cut my nuts off. I wasn't entirely sure what I'd done to warrant it, but I was going to find out.

That's for damn sure.

"*Please*. I need to talk to her."

"She went to an early dinner with"—Rachel smirked before finishing her sentence—"a date."

Fire spread through my veins. Wow, it had only been a week, and she was already dating? The thought of someone else touching her, kissing her, made me want to throw her over my shoulder and show her I was the only one who could make her body come alive.

"Where. Is. She?" I gritted out.

Rachel grinned. "If I tell you, what are you going to do?"

"March in there and tell her she belongs with me."

"Good. Make sure you do just that."

Once I left the office, I stalked into the restaurant where Rachel had said Brittney and her *date* were. A growl left my lips when I spotted her sitting at a table. She sat with a man who had inches and at least fifty pounds on me. By the looks of his high-end tailored dress slacks, pressed shirt, and the watch that probably cost more than my car was worth, it was clear he had money too.

So this was what she wanted? A man with money? Or did she want the buff, muscular type?

She threw her head back and laughed at something the prick said, and my feet were moving before I even realized.

When I stopped at her table and she looked up, her eyes went round.

Fuck, I missed that.

Brittney

"Derek," I started, surprised. I smiled once my shock wore off. I couldn't help it; I missed him. But then I noticed the intensity in his gaze and panicked a little. "Wh—what are you doing here?"

"I could ask you the same question," he said, gesturing to Jackson, who sat across the table from me. "Is this what you want? A muscle head with money?"

I placed my hand on Jackson's arm before he could stand and punch Derek. Not that I thought he would. Jackson had too much self-control. But he could be intimidating when he needed to be.

Jackson's gaze met mine. "So, this is Derek? The douche who left without saying a word in Lake Tahoe?"

I cringed. "Yes."

"Can I punch him now?" He smirked.

I rolled my eyes at his protectiveness, then turned my attention back to the seething man standing next to the table. "Derek," I said, looking back up, "I'd like you to meet my *brother*, Jackson."

"Your—" His gaze swiveled from Jackson back to me. "Your brother?"

"Yes, my *brother*."

I fought back a chuckle at his expression. His impulsiveness and dramatics always made me laugh. How I attracted these people was beyond me.

"Rachel said you were on a date."

I rolled my eyes. Of course she would say that. Just couldn't leave well enough alone, could she?

"Well, I'm not. So again, I ask, what are you doing here?"

He closed his eyes and ran a hand down his face. "I wanted to talk to you."

"So let me get this straight. You thought I was on a date and decided you needed to talk to me so urgently that it would be alright to interrupt?"

He narrowed his eyes at me before he answered. "Yes, because the thought of you with someone else made me crazy."

My eyes widened at his admission. What was he trying to say?

Jackson laughed before standing and placing his hand on Derek's shoulder. "Only because I can relate, I'll give you a pass. But if you hurt her again, I'll find you. Got it?"

"Again?" I heard Derek mutter.

"I'm assuming I'll see you at Thanksgiving next week." Jackson leaned down toward me and placed a quick kiss on my cheek. "Go easy on him. You women make us lose our minds."

I rolled my eyes, knowing he was talking about his own situation just as much as Derek's. But I still didn't understand what Derek wanted.

After Jackson left, the man in question sat across from me. "Liam and Hunter offered me the position here permanently."

I leaned back and folded my arms across my chest. So, what? He wanted me to know he'd still be my boss? Did he think this meant we would go back to what we were doing before? I had too much self-respect to be used just because it was convenient, and I had every intention of telling him just that.

"What does that have to do with me?"

"It has everything to do with you. I asked Liam two weeks ago if there was a way I could stay."

What? I sat up straighter. "You did?" I didn't want to hope it was *for* us. For a *real* us. I needed him to say it. "Why? Why did you want to stay?"

He reached both hands across the table and grasped mine. "Because the thought of leaving you killed me. I hoped you felt the same, but when you said you wanted to end things, I—"

"I didn't *want* to end things," I interjected. "Hunter was coming back. I thought you were going back to Nashville and things were going to end anyway. It was making me sick. I thrive in my box of concrete and routine, and I couldn't handle having our inevitable end hanging over us." It was the truth. I would never be like Savannah.

He stared at my hands, his voice low, vulnerable. "I didn't want to get your hopes up until Liam confirmed it. And when you ended things, I was blindsided." He looked up, the hope I felt mirrored in his eyes. "But if we're being honest, I can't stay and not be with you. It would be too hard. I understand if you don't feel the same."

Whoa. He really wants this? Us? He'd gone out on a limb, admitting how he felt, and now it was my turn to be brave.

Finally, I uttered the only thought I could form the words for. "I would need to draw up papers."

"Papers?"

"Yeah, disclosing our relationship and signing away rights to sue Hunter or Liam if shit goes sideways." I smiled when his eyebrows raised.

"I'd sign my soul away if it meant we could be together."

I wanted to tease him for his dramatics once again, but the giddy feeling that settled over me left me speechless.

My cheeks heated as I leaned across the table. "Want to get out of here, then?"

His smirk told me he understood what I was getting at. "What did you have in mind?"

"Your place is a quick walk from here."

Without a word, he stood. Still holding my hand, he practically pulled me out of the restaurant. I giggled as we walked quickly to his loft.

It didn't take long for us to get naked; we didn't even make it to the bedroom. He had me pinned against the wall just inside his door. I wanted to sink down on him when he lined himself up to my entrance, but he held me against the wall, keeping me in place.

"Fuck," he mumbled near my ear. "We need a condom."

I grabbed him tightly by the shoulders, stopping him from stepping back. "I'm on the pill. Please Derek, I need you now."

"You sure? I'm clean. I haven't—"

"I'm sure. Stop talking. Need to feel you," I panted.

He entered me in one thrust, and we moaned in unison. It felt so good. So right. It was hard and fast; we were so desperate for each other. Like we were pouring every thought, every emotion, every word we hadn't yet said into the moment.

After we had showered and then gone for round two, I lay next to him with my head on his chest as he ran his fingers through my hair.

I wanted to tell him I was in love with him. But was it too soon? This all felt fast. None of the relationships I'd been in before had moved this quickly.

"Will you come to Boston with me next week? To visit my family? We can wait until Friday to leave. I know you have family coming on Thanksgiving Day."

I leaned up on my elbow to look at him. "You don't think that's all too fast? Meeting the families?"

He rolled me onto my back, pinning me to the mattress.

"I'm moving here to be with you. I'm so in love with you that I can't imagine not being with you. I think meeting each other's families is appropriate."

I smiled up at him as he kissed my nose.

"You love me?"

He rolled his eyes with a chuckle. "I thought that part was obvious." He turned serious again. His cock, hard again already, breaching my entrance.

"I love you too," I said with a moan as he thrust inside me.

Jesus. He might kill me yet with his stamina.

18

DEREK

OVER THE LAST MONTH, things had moved quickly between Brittney and me. And now we were spending the weekend in Brittney's hometown, Half Moon Lake. There was an annual Christmas party at a place called The Dock that included Brittney's family, Savannah's family and a few others.

I met and spent Thanksgiving with her family. Her brother Jackson gave me a hard time, but I liked the guy. Brittney and I spent a few days after that in Boston. My family loved her, and she and my mom became fast friends.

Jackson arranged for my client and her partner to visit the kids at the children's hospital. He was pissed at first when he figured out our angle. But when Brittney said the client would donate a generous amount, he couldn't say no. He might look like a big tough guy, but Brittney said he has a heart ten times the size of anyone she knows.

We also made another big move. I had been renting my loft on a month-to-month basis, and her apartment was affordable and spacious. So I moved in with her. We soon started looking at places to buy. We really wanted a brownstone, and we'd toured two earlier in the week but hadn't made a decision yet.

Right now, I was content to hold her in my arms as we danced to the music. I brushed my lips against hers, and when the smell of jasmine hit my nose, my dick twitched against her hip. I bought her a couple bottles of her favorite lotion for Christmas. Needed to make sure she never ran out.

Brittney giggled. "Seriously?"

"What?" I asked sheepishly. "I can't help that I find you so irresistible." We danced a little more before I nodded to her brother and a blonde having a heated discussion. "What's up with that?"

She glanced over and her mouth turned down. "I don't know. He's been closed off about it in the last week or so. It's a mess. I hope it gets resolved soon. I hate seeing him hurting."

"Liam is the closest thing I've ever had to a brother, so I don't really know what it's like to have a sibling."

"Savannah has four of them, five if you include Bella"— she pointed to a short brunette holding a toddler—"who's pretty much been a Williams her whole life. And Savannah complains about all of them daily. But I haven't figured out why they all drive her nuts."

"And Savannah's brother Rhett is the one who's married to Bella, right? And they're expecting?"

"Yeah, she's so cute. She's practically glowing already."

"You want kids?"

Shit. Didn't mean to just throw that out there. But I saw how her face lit up when Savannah came to visit last week and told her Bella had announced their pregnancy to the family.

She chuckled. "Oh, so we're having *that* conversation now?"

I shrugged. "Just curious."

More than curious. I wanted a big family. I was an only child, and I didn't want that for my own kids. And I really hoped we were on the same page.

"I do. Eventually. I want to travel a bit first."

"Me too. Maybe two years?"

Her eyes went wide, and I bit back a groan. Those big brown eyes of hers would be my undoing. I was sure of it.

"You're the one who likes to plan everything, remember? How the hell I'm going to propose to you without you trying to figure out every detail is beyond me."

She just shrugged. "Sorry not sorry?"

I laughed. At least she could admit her faults. Her being a planner and not liking surprises were flaws I was happy to deal with. Just like how she put up with me when I left my socks all over the floor.

But in all the ways that mattered, we were perfect for each other.

And I couldn't wait to get her back to Lake Tahoe and propose. I figured the place that brought us together should be the place I asked her to spend the rest of her life with me.

After all, the wish I made there had come true.

Want to see more of Half Moon Lake?
Click here to start the series now!

***

Keep reading for a sneak peek at Always Yours!

CHAPTER ONE

Bella

I glanced down at the long fingers threaded through mine. My gaze traveled from our clasped hands resting on my knee, up to Rhett's muscular forearm. I didn't remember when he'd rolled the sleeves of his pressed white dress shirt to his elbows, but it had been an excruciatingly long day. It was hard to believe that less than eight weeks ago, my mom and I were shopping for dresses for the fall homecoming dance and now... now...

"Bella?" Miranda softly repeated, still hovering over me.

I forced my eyes to meet hers. "I'm sorry. What were you saying?"

Her eyes glistened with a sheen of tears.

Please, no. Not you too.

Between the funeral and the reception at our home, I had no more tears left to cry.

"Can I get you something to eat?" she asked again, this time crouching down in front of me. Her son Rhett and I were sitting on the sofa in my living room. The exact spot my mom and I had spent plenty of nights curled up, watching movies.

"No, thanks." I shook my head. The thought of food made me queasy.

Miranda hesitated for a second, then her gaze turned to her son. "You know she'll only listen to you, so try and get her to eat something?"

"Yeah, Mom. I'll try." Rhett eyed me while giving my hand a tight squeeze.

I stole a glance his way, expecting him to convince me to eat. His jaw clenched as his eyes searched my face. I knew he felt helpless, fussing over me all day. Trying to fix my pain. But there wasn't a fix, and the look of vulnerability on his tanned face constricted my chest in a completely different kind of ache. He had been my best friend for as long as I could remember. I think my mom knew I would need him now more than ever.

"Bella bug, you and Rhett have that special bond." She reached *for my hand as she struggled to speak. "It's a once in a lifetime type of thing. Cherish it."* Her coughs overtook her before she continued. *"Protect it. Fight for it when you need to, because I promise you baby girl..."* Another cough and shallow breath as she whispered, *"Nothing that special will ever come easy."*

That was a week ago, while her frail body struggled to fight off the pneumonia.

Rhett's warm breath against my ear pulled me back to the present, and I inhaled sharply. I found comfort in it. A reprieve from the pain I had felt all day.

"Do you want to go for a walk?" he tentatively asked.

I glanced around the room full of people to search out my father's tall, lean frame. "Sure, just let me tell my dad. I don't want him to worry."

My eyes landed on him as he ran one hand nervously through his thick chocolate-brown hair. He was speaking to a familiar elderly woman, one of many who had come to pay their respects.

"Bella Buchanan." She reached out and cupped my cheek. "My, how beautiful you are. Looking more and more like your mother every day. We will miss her dearly; she was always as bright and exquisite as those flowers in her shop."

The ripple of pain that swept over me made it even harder to breathe.

I need to get out of here. Now.

"Thank you, Mrs. Adams," I said politely before I turned toward my dad, Allen, and continued with, "I'm going to get a little air. Is that alright?"

Worry clouded his dark eyes. "Is Rhett going with you?"

"Yes, we won't be long."

"Okay," he said to me before turning and addressing my best friend. "Rhett, make sure she eats something, please."

How do they expect me to eat when everything hurts?

"Yes, Mr. Buchanan, I will."

As we made our way through the large eat-in kitchen, Rhett grabbed a premade sandwich from the tray and two bottles of water. We headed toward the well-worn path that led from our property down to the lake. Even though it wasn't waterfront property like Rhett's family's, my mom had picked this home because she loved the foliage and the view of Half Moon Lake. Our small town was tucked into the North Carolina mountains, along a large lake shaped like a crescent. Hence, how it got its name.

We sat on a large rock near the water. Rhett handed me the sandwich he'd grabbed and one of the bottles.

"Eat," he ordered with a look that said *do not argue with me.* I reluctantly forced the sandwich down and prayed it didn't come back up. Usually, I preferred avocado and bacon on a turkey sandwich, but today I didn't care. Everything tasted like sandpaper to me.

After sitting in silence, Rhett surprised me by wrapping his arm around my shoulders and pulling me tight into his side. I rested my head on his chest and tried to focus on the small laps of water against the shore. Usually, the rhythmic sound was soothing, but the pressure within me refused to quiet down. I didn't want to cry, but before I knew it, tears were streaming down my face.

"Shh, I'm here. I got you," he said softly as one hand cradled my head to his chest. The other soothingly rubbed my arm.

"It's—not—fair. Why did this happen? Why did she have to leave me?" I sobbed.

I tilted my head up to look into Rhett's normally bright blue eyes that were now a cool gray, standing out against his naturally tan skin tone and dark hair.

His gaze was like a cloudy sky in winter, and I pulled back with an inaudible gasp. The way he looked at me was drastically different from the look of pity from almost everyone else that day. I could tell that he felt all the pain I was feeling as well. It surprised me that we could be real with each other, and I didn't have to put up a front with him.

"I don't know, Bella. But I'm here, and I promise you I won't ever leave you," he muttered as his lips brushed against my forehead. He was so sweet, and I was so lucky that he treated me with the same love and care he treated his sisters with.

And yet, the past summer was the first time I started thinking about Rhett as anything more than just a friend. Between helping his dad at the marina and being on the high school football team, I would have had to be blind to miss his newly formed muscles.

Stop it, Bella. Not now.

But he was a senior with his pick of pretty popular girls, and I was a sophomore. Next year he would be off at college, and he looked at me as nothing more than another little sister. Rhett's lean, muscular frame was the *last* thing I should be thinking about.

"You can't promise that, and besides, you're leaving for college next fall," I responded after pausing a moment too long. A wave of dread swept over me at the thought of Rhett not being there.

He chuckled. "You know what I meant. College is temporary, and I'll be back for holidays and every summer."

But my mom's illness was only supposed to be temporary.

With his arm still firmly secured around my shoulder, the silence engulfed us until he asked, "Are you ready to head back?"

"No," I muttered. "Can we sit like this for a little while longer?"

"Of course. You know I would do anything for you," he admitted a bit sheepishly. Was he blushing? No, that didn't make sense. It must have been the wind picking up, warming his cheeks.

At that moment, I realized just how true my mom's words were. Our friendship might not always be easy, but I would do whatever it took to never lose it.

If we could get through what was bound to be one of the worst days of my life, surely we could handle anything...right?

***

Want to see more of Half Moon Lake?
Click <u>here </u>to start the series now!

***

A NOTE FROM THE AUTHOR

Dear Reader,

THANK YOU for reading *Wishing to Be Yours*. I hope you enjoyed this fun, steamy office romance. This book was originally planned for next year. But when I got the opportunity to join The Silver Lining series, I knew Brittney and Derek's story would be perfect for it!

I appreciate each and every one of you. It's only because people like you read our books that authors like me get to publish them. I never imagined I'd be writing a Dear Reader, let alone a second one!

Want to see more of Half Moon Lake? Keep reading for an inside look at Always Yours, book one in the Half Moon Lake series, and a sneak peek at Goldilocks and the Grumpy Bear coming December 1, 2022. A quick holiday read and a new spin on nursery rhymes that I'm co-writing with my author bestie Jenni Bara.

Check out my website for bonus content and if you've already read Always Yours, watch for the pre-order of the next book in the series. Can you guess who it is? I know you all are so ready for this one! Stay tuned!

Love, AJ Ranney
www.ajranney.com

Turn the page for the First Chapter of Always Yours, book one in the Half Moon Lake series.

Always Yours
Now Available on Amazon & KU

START THE HALF MOON LAKE SERIES

GOLDILOCKS AND THE GRUMPY BEAR

SNEAK PEEK

DECLAN

"Lauren, why do you always have to be such a—" Declan couldn't finish the sentence before the phone fell from his hand. His body moved without permission because a small blonde was falling from the sky. Years of instinct kicked in as he moved into position to catch her.

Her pointy elbow smacked hard into the apple of his cheek as his hand slid to grab her upper thigh. Instead of letting him catch her, like a normal fucking person, she thrashed and fought like he was the problem, causing them both to teeter. He swallowed a grunt as he slammed into the hardwood, taking the brunt of the fall and hitting the ground with an umph just as her body landed hard on top of him.

"Don't touch me!" the crazed lune shouted.

"I'm trying to help you, lady. Stop flailing around." He pinned her arms to her sides, forcing her to still and leaving her awkwardly pressed to his chest. He just needed a second to regroup and chill this woman out. Walking into his house and having a person fall out of the sky had shaken up his plans for the day.

"Mom?" Declan's son Chris crowed behind him. "No, he pulled some naked lady on top of him, and now they're laying on the floor."

Jesus. That was not what happened.

His ex was controlling and possessive to the extreme, which were two of the many reasons he and Lauren hadn't worked out. But because ball bunnies had done crazy shit during his time as a major league baseball player, Lauren was always a watchdog about his time with Chris. This stunt today, though, took the cake. Crashing his son's Christmas vacation in a skimpy robe crossed too many lines for Declan to even process.

If his agent had let his whereabouts slip again, he'd find himself out of a job. The last thing he wanted was for his ex to drive up here and steal their son back. Plus, this woman wasn't even naked.

But now that he was looking, her robe had ridden up to reveal a tight ass covered in a scrap of lace. Great. Just what he needed. He grabbed the robe—if anyone could call the short, silky material that—and yanked it down over her ass. He didn't need to scar his six-year-old.

As soon as he released her arms, she shot up like a rocket, straddling his right leg.

"You better let me go." She balled one hand into a fist with the thumb tucked under her fingers while she struggled to hold her robe together with the other. The woman didn't even know how to punch without breaking her thumb.

Nothing about this woman screamed ball bunny. Although the outfit was aggressive, there was something shy and modest about her demeanor, and the soft lavender scent was the exact opposite of the cloying perfume most bunnies he'd met wore. He was starting to feel like a perv for staring at the soft swell of her breasts against the satin fabric. It was hot, especially the way she was straddling his leg.

Jesus, idiot. Stop it.

He shook his head. His son was ten feet behind him, his ex on the other end of phone—no doubt more pissed than she had been when they were arguing two minutes prior, and he was not letting himself get turned on by the crazy ball bunny who'd broken into his house.

He sighed as she pulled her fist back.

"Okay, listen, I'm trying to be a nice guy, but I'm going to have to call the police if you hit me again."

"Again?" She cocked her head, and her eyebrows pulled together. But her utter confusion gave him a moment to extract himself from below her and get to his feet.

"Here, give me the phone, Chris." He held his hand out to his son.

"Oh, Mom hung up." Chris shrugged. "She sounded angry."

I bet she did.

Thank God the blizzard would keep her from driving up here to add to this crazy.

"I thought you were supposed to be good at catching things, Dad. How'd you miss the naked lady so badly?"

Declan closed his eyes again, trying not to laugh. "I catch baseballs. Not wet noodles falling from the sky."

A huff came from the wet noodle as she slammed her hands on her hips. "I thought we weren't allowed to climb on the kitchen counters," Chris accused.

Was it too much to ask for a few low-key days with his kid? One week. That was all he asked. He hated the cold and didn't really want to be here. But his son wanted a white Christmas, and he would do anything for Chris.

"We're not." Declan narrowed his eyes. "Not sure why Goldilocks here was standing on the counters."

"Like Goldilocks and the three bears?" Chris widened his eyes, flicking his gaze from his dad to the woman. "Is that why she's here? To eat all our food and sleep in our beds?"

"No!" Please don't let Chris say that to his mother. "She's not doing that. Now, look, lady. Why don't you tell me how you broke in and why you're climbing on my kitchen counters."

"Broke in? Are you kidding me?" She crossed her arms under her breasts, giving him a glimpse of cleavage as the robe shifted open at the top.

"I promise you; I am not. I don't joke around." Declan struggled to keep his focus centered on her face—nowhere lower—because apparently crazy really did turn him on. After years with Lauren, it shouldn't have surprised him that crazy was his type, but he refused to go down that road again. He'd learned the hard way what a headache it would be. A headache he'd lived with for years and wouldn't shake for a long, long time.

"You gave me the key."

"Really, Dad?" Chris asked. Now he had his hands on his hips too.

"No." He spun to his son, shaking his head. "No, I did not give her a key."

This was all he needed. His son saying, "Hey, Mom. Dad gave a half-naked Goldilocks keys to his house to surprise him." Shit. She'd have a field day with that, and he'd get even less time with his son.

"What idiot doesn't know when he rents his own house out?" Goldilocks huffed but spun away from him.

What was she talking about? He definitely hadn't rented out his house this week.

"I'm not arguing with you. This is my house, and it was not available this week."

"Dad, can't underwear lady just stay here with us?"

"No!" Goldilocks and Declan said in unison before turning back to glare at each other.

"This is ridiculous. I'm leaving. And expect a horrible review on Airbnb, Finn," she hissed out.

She stomped past him, leaving him standing in the kitchen as what she said hit him.

Finn. Oh no.

He dialed his brother, but before Finn could say hello he snapped out, "Why is there a crazy chick in my house?"

"How would I know? Why would you invite a ball bunny on your trip to Florida with Chris?"

"I'm at the cabin in New York."

"Oh—well—then maybe I could answer that." Finn chuckled.

You've got to be kidding me.

Want more Declan & Chris Order Now!!

Goldilocks and the Grumpy Bear

ACKNOWLEDGMENTS

First and foremost, I need to thank my husband. He has been one of my biggest cheerleaders, is always willing to listen to what I write, and has done bedtime with the kids more times than I probably realize. I appreciate your eagerness to help me when I'm stuck and your willingness to let me read to you.

And then to my kids, who have been curious about what Mommy is writing and have tried so very hard to be patient and understanding every time I've had to tell them I need to work on my book. I hope when they're teenagers they still think it's cool.

Thank you to my mom, who has been so supportive, always asking questions about the process and telling me how proud she is of me. And even dealing with my mood swings when I'm overwhelmed.

To my mother-in-law, thank you for being excited about this, listening to me ramble, and also telling me how proud you are.

Jenn, I don't even have words to thank you for all you've done, but I will try. I know if I hadn't found you when I did, I would have given up. It has been you every step of the way who, in your own way, encouraged me to grow and learn. You're always willing to read and edit multiple times, hold my hand when I need it, and tell me to just do it when I need that too. But above everything you've done, your friendship has meant the world to me. I can't wait to go on this crazy journey *together*. Oh, and thank you for ALL the millions of phone calls.

Holly, as always, thank you for being my sister, even if not by blood. Your support has always meant so much, and this has been no different.

Amanda, let's be honest, no one would be reading these words without your initial encouragement when I told you about my dream and interest in writing a book.

Matt, thanks for letting me pick your brain and for your excitement about a book you'll likely never read.

Katie, you are amazing. Thank you for reading and for your amazing feedback!

A HUGE thank you to my author friends who have supported me in so many ways, whether it was just encouragement or reading my stuff: Annie Charme, Kat Long, Raleigh Damson, Jenni Bara, and many more!

Beth, thank you for being so flexible, your edits, and the millions of questions and emails.

Haley, thank you for all the many ways you assist me. From graphics to sharing and promoting and all the stuff you likely will do that I just don't know yet. Making things easy for me so I can focus on writing.

And finally, thank you to the rest of my friends and family who have helped or supported me. I used to think it takes a village to raise little humans, and that still holds true, but it also takes a village to write and publish a book!

ABOUT THE AUTHOR

A.J. Ranney lives in Maryland with her ever-growing zoo, including two kids, two cats, an attention-loving dog, a bunny, a cricket-eating lizard and her lovable, well-meaning husband.

She likes to leave the chaos of her real world behind and lose herself in a steamy romance novel. Her passion for reading romance prompted her writing journey, leading her to create relatable happily ever afters that come from her own dreams and experiences.

She loves coffee, sushi, wine, and her family. Not necessarily in that order. Her inner peace comes from the water, always relating to her zodiac sign, the Pisces. It's no wonder the small town she created in her stories is situated on a lake.